RED ALERT

*Other B&W titles*
*by Margaret Thomson Davis*

THE BREADMAKERS SAGA
THE NEW BREADMAKERS
THE CLYDESIDERS TRILOGY
THE TOBACCO LORDS TRILOGY
A DARKENING OF THE HEART
THE DARK SIDE OF PLEASURE
BURNING AMBITION
THE GLASGOW BELLE
LIGHT AND DARK
WRITE FROM THE HEART
A DEADLY DECEPTION
GOODMANS OF GLASSFORD STREET

MARGARET THOMSON
DAVIS

# RED ALERT

B & W PUBLISHING

First published 2008
by Black & White Publishing Ltd
29 Ocean Drive, Edinburgh EH6 6JL

1 3 5 7 9 10 8 6 4 2    08 09 10 11

ISBN: 978 1 84502 221 1



A CIP catalogue record for this book is available from
the British Library.



Typeset by RefineCatch Limited, Bungay, Suffolk

Printed and bound by MPG Books Ltd

## ACKNOWLEDGEMENTS

Special thanks to my son, Kenneth Baillie Davis, who, because he took his degree at the Rennie Mackintosh School of Art, was able to help and advise me about the scenes in the art school.

The sexy poetry in the book was supplied by my old friend Michael Malone whose books of poetry are always worth buying.

My gratitude and admiration goes to all the members of the Fire and Rescue Service who helped and advised me while I was writing *Red Alert*.

# DEDICATION

I dedicate this book with heartfelt thanks to the two Marys – Mary Ferguson who has not only been an excellent home help but a kind and loyal friend, and to Mary Brown who has also been a kind, supportive and loyal friend.

# I

Kirsty Price wished her father was dead. She watched Simon Price's solid, rangy build and bald head silhouetted against the stained-glass window in the front door, before he opened the door and lumbered down the steps on to Botanic Crescent and into his big four-by-four. She hoped, prayed even, as she did every morning, that he would be killed in a car crash on his way to work. She could just imagine how he would be making his students suffer in the Glasgow School of Art, with his exaggerated glances and snide, sarcastic comments. She often felt like killing him and she had no doubt some of them did too.

It was how he had treated her young brother that made her really hate him. He would never let up with his constant nagging and belittling of everything Johnny did. Nothing Johnny did could ever live up to his expectations or please him. She worried about her young brother. He was so vulnerable and unable to cope. Johnny had suffered ill health for most of his twenty-one years. He had been a delicate, premature baby and then, at fifteen, he had developed agonising rheumatic fever. That illness had left him with a heart condition. He had also suffered terrible ulcers in his mouth and had to have all his teeth removed. He had always been acutely embarrassed and ashamed at having to wear dentures at his age.

'You're a right idiot, hanging about outside the GOMA with your freaky Goth pals, all dolled up in black and pins and chains, and purple lipstick,' her father accused.

Her mother would always try to come to Johnny's defence.

'Simon, he's not doing anybody any harm, and he can't help his health problem. The valves of his heart . . .'

She never managed to get very far.

'He's twenty-one years of age and still a financial burden.'

'Dad,' Johnny desperately interrupted. 'I've got a job.'

'How long'll this job last, I wonder. Your last effort didn't last long.' Simon's thick moustache jutting aggressively, he turned to his daughter to sneer, 'We'll just have to depend on our clever wee dish-washer to make a contribution.'

Kirsty had found a job in the kitchen of the nearby fire station, making breakfast and lunch for the firefighters. Her father was always making a fool of the job and saying she hadn't enough brains to go to university. But the job meant she could get home in plenty of time to be with her mother and make sure she took the afternoon rest in bed that the doctor had ordered. Her mother had developed angina, which wasn't surprising, living such a stressful life.

Her mother adored Johnny and suffered agonies every time Simon attacked him. She had always been such a gentle, caring woman.

Johnny took after his mother. He didn't have a bad or resentful bone in his body. He was tall and thin, with a shock of fair curly hair and large, eager-to-please blue eyes. He'd dyed his hair black but his eyes were just the same as they'd always been.

'Mummy's blue-eyed boy,' Simon always sneered.

Johnny had tried different jobs and had made enough to buy a second-hand Mini, which he hoped to customise. It was a horrible sickly shade of yellow and his father made a terrible fool of it, but it didn't spoil Johnny's pride and pleasure in owning it. His last job had been working in a café in town. However, the varying shifts and the fact that the business of the café meant he was continually on his feet and under pressure had caused him yet again to lose his job.

There were a couple of regular customers that he'd become particularly friendly with. They always had a pleasant bit of banter with him, which made his shift go slightly more quickly. He was rather taken with them – with their air of sophistication and poise. He was flattered by their interest in him. Kirsty found the attention they were giving him rather strange. Polite chit-chat and friendly interest were a sign of a good tipping customer, but she began to wonder about their motives. She didn't like to think that way, but she couldn't help being suspicious.

They were a glamorous-looking pair called Renee and Paul Henley, and so different from Johnny with his Goth look. Kirsty had voiced her unease to her mother.

'Och, you're a right wee worrier, Kirsty. You're worse than me. Renee and Paul seem very nice, kind people. Johnny thinks the world of them.'

'I know that, Mum. But why are they taking such an interest in Johnny, I wonder? I mean, they're so different from him.'

Her mother was contentedly stroking Jingles, the cat, so called because of the tiny bell that dangled from its collar.

'They think the world of Johnny. And why not? He's a lovely boy. This Goth thing's just a stage he's going through.'

Still, Kirsty kept thinking, Paul and Renee were both very worldly-wise and sophisticated compared with her naive young brother. They both worked as croupiers in the casino. She had met them briefly in Byres Road while she was out shopping with Johnny. He had introduced them excitedly. Kirsty had used the opportunity to quiz them in as casual a tone as possible.

'Isn't there a café or a restaurant in the casino?'

'Oh yes, and I could get free tea and coffee. But it's good to get out and have a break from the place.'

It was understandable, she supposed. But now they were saying that the job in the café was too much for Johnny. Carrying heavy trays of dishes was bound to be putting a strain on his heart. No doubt that was true. Nevertheless, it seemed odd, to say the least, that Paul and Renee had offered him a job looking after their flat in Byres Road.

'Johnny tells me you've offered him some sort of job. We're certainly glad he won't be staying unemployed. It's very kind of you.'

'We work such long hours,' Renee explained, 'and it worries us that our flat is left empty and unattended so much. There've been so many burglaries in and around the West End recently.'

Perhaps that was perfectly reasonable. And yet . . .

Kirsty tried very hard not to be suspicious and to be pleased for Johnny. He was so delighted.

'It's not far from here, only a few minutes' walk, and I'll really enjoy keeping an eye on the flat and having a nice meal prepared for Renee and Paul to warm up when they get home.'

The fire station where Kirsty worked was just about as handy as Renee and Paul's place, only in the opposite direction. At first, Kirsty had been shy and withdrawn in the company of the firefighters, but they very soon put her at her ease. She absolutely loved working in the place and she admired the firefighters beyond words.

The small kitchen upstairs was part of the large day room, with a hatch through which she could serve the meals. The men, muscles bulging under their black trousers and black T-shirts, and the open-necked black shirts they sometimes wore on top, formed a noisy, cheerful queue. When it was time for a mid-morning tea or coffee, they often persuaded her to join them at the long table. The men were always cheery or cheeky, a flirtatious comment given with a grin.

If she wasn't busy, or even while she was cooking or washing-up, she liked to watch the firefighters work out on the fitness machines that were positioned down one side of the room. It was very necessary to keep fit for such a dangerous and heavy job.

Today, she was watching the men as they worked out, paying special attention to Greg McFarlane as he pumped his arms through a set of bicep curls. His muscles flexed and bulged as he grunted out his final reps. He was framed by two other firefighters performing shoulder presses. She smiled to herself – it was like having her own private performance by the Chippendales. Greg came over to the hatch, rubbing the sweat from his face, neck and hard, muscly arms with a towel.

'Stop fussing about in there, Kirsty. Come out and relax for a few minutes. Have a coffee with me.'

There were already other firefighters sitting at the table having their morning coffee, and they greeted her with, 'Hey there, blondie.'

She joined them shyly but gladly. She liked all of them but Greg was her favourite. She put a cup of coffee down in front of him, then sat beside him at the table. Today he was on red watch. There was a continual rota of four watches – red, green, white and blue; two day shifts and two night shifts. The day shifts were from eight in the morning until six at night. The night shift ran from six at night until eight in the morning. Seventeen firefighters belonged to the station, and they were all wonderful men, in her opinion, but none more so than Greg. She was always thankful when he was on day duty.

His policeman friend was at the table with him today, notebook in front of him. Sergeant Jack Campbell from the local police office was writing a history of the fire service in his spare time.

'Listen,' Greg was saying to her now, 'we're both off duty this evening. If you're not doing anything else, how about us meeting up and going to the pictures? Or for a meal, or just a drink. Whatever you like.'

She felt flattered and sad at the same time.

'I'm sorry, Greg. I'd love to but my mother doesn't keep too well and . . .'

'Isn't there anyone else living at home?'

'Yes, my father and my brother.'

'Well then. You deserve some time off to relax and enjoy yourself. Go on, say you'll come.'

'Aye, go on,' Jack Campbell laughed, 'put him out of his misery.'

Before she could give any more excuses, the bell electrified the air, and Greg and the other men – except for Jack Campbell – made for the door, knocking chairs over in their rush, their boots making a thunderous clatter.

She could see in her mind's eye how he and the other firefighters rushed along the corridor. Reaching the poles, they swung out, spinning and swooping down to the firm rubber mat below. Some landed on their feet and in one smooth motion raced for the fire engine. Others mistimed their landing in their hurry, landed harshly but immediately rolled over and up with hardly a break in speed. They swung up through the cabin doors as the driver revved the engine. The huge truck was already in motion as the doors slammed closed.

'Great guys,' Jack Campbell said, and Kirsty heartily agreed with him. She prayed that they would be safely back before she went off duty. But when the time came for her to go, the shift had still not reappeared. She had to leave in an agony of anxiety. It was always like this now. She couldn't bear the thought of anything happening to Greg.

She determined to spend as much time as she could listening for the sound of the fire engine returning along Queen Margaret Drive and watching from the window for the sight of it. Botanic Crescent, where the family's terraced house was situated, was just off Queen Margaret Drive and the fire engine would have to pass the end of the Crescent. Unless, of course, the fire had been at the other side of the city.

It was while she was trying to keep looking out and listening for the fire engine that her mother said, 'Johnny is very excited about this new idea of Paul's.'

'What new idea?'

'I'm not sure, dear. It seems to be a bit hush-hush at this early stage. But Johnny's very excited about it.'

Kirsty didn't like the hush-hush bit. It sounded to her as if there could be something dishonest about it. Johnny was so easily manipulated and persuaded, he would be an easy target for the likes of Renee and Paul Henley. As soon as Johnny arrived home, she would question him and find out what the pair were trying to get him up to.

Just then, her mother switched on the television and the screen filled with the ominous orange glow of the fire, the silhouettes of the fire crew in stark contrast to the inferno behind. The reporter's voice gave a steady commentary above the background noise of the roaring, crackling furnace. There had been an explosion in the kitchen of a first-floor restaurant in Argyle Street. Kirsty heard the reporter talking to the camera, telling of the fears that people were trapped inside. In the background, she saw firefighters, anonymous in their bulky breathing apparatus, disappearing into the smoke and flames that enveloped the building. Kirsty felt sick. It was then she realised how much Greg meant to her. Her father had always spoiled, indeed ruined, the few relationships she'd had in the past – even female friendships. This time, if God spared Greg and helped him to survive this latest conflagration safely, she would defy her father and say yes to Greg.

Her father wouldn't succeed in ruining this chance of happiness. She'd see him dead first.

# 2

From Sauchiehall Street, a steep hill had to be climbed in order to reach the Glasgow School of Art, which loomed large like a medieval castle proudly straddling the crest of the hill. The entrance in Renfrew Street was fronted by a curving slope of steps, wide at the front and gradually narrowing. The entrance was topped by two elongated figures acting as guardians, each holding a vase and facing a rose bush with its flowers growing clear above its leaves.

Underneath were the Mackintosh doors with their distinctive motif. Above the entrance stretched the Director's balcony, and higher still, the studio with its slated roof. This was no ordinary place. No other building anywhere could compare with it. Even the ironwork and railings were startlingly novel and complex, with pierced metal discs rising through clusters of leaves. This school was not only the masterpiece of its creator, Charles Rennie Mackintosh, but so gloriously original that people came from all over the world to experience it.

Sandra Matheson pushed the doors back and entered the ground-floor hall. The open-fronted shop was on her left and she immediately spotted Tommy Pratt. Every time she thought of his name, she felt sorry for him. You had to be really tough to survive the torment that was sure to be meted out because of the name Pratt, and Tommy was not tough. He was an immensely talented and sensitive young man. She admired his talent and loved him dearly. He had been studying a large book about Charles Rennie Mackintosh but, glancing up, he saw her and smiled. Then he put the book down, picked up his portfolio and came towards her.

'Hi.'

'Hi.' She went on tiptoe and kissed him. 'You OK?'

He smiled ruefully.

'I felt fine until I came in here.'

She knew what he meant. It wasn't the building or meeting up with other students. Only one person made his life hell and that was one of their art tutors, Simon Price. He wasn't the only student who suffered, of course, but the name Pratt gave the tutor an extra edge to his twisted sense of humour.

They clattered up the wide wooden staircase, emerging from the pool of shade that was the atrium into the luminous light that flooded the museum, which was peppered with casts, paintings and sculpture. Rennie Mackintosh had purposely designed it to have different areas of light and dark. Through the studio door with its ornate brass plate and number, they saw some of the other students already there. Friendly greetings were exchanged. Soon all the easels had been set up, and Simon Price arrived and stood chatting to the model who stood, hands on hips, confident and at ease, although he was clothed only in a towel tied around his narrow, athletic waist. The model told them during one of the breaks that he was a full-time firefighter but was doing the modelling to earn a bit of extra cash.

He was a tall man with hard-looking muscles and when he dropped the towel, it was obvious that he was well endowed in the genital area as well. Sandra felt no embarrassment at having to stare at the man's naked body and study every detail of it. Nor, it seemed, did any of the other students. Everyone was concentrating on conveying the man accurately and artistically onto canvas.

The man's name was Greg, Greg McFarlane. She'd once said to him, 'I think you ought to have been a policeman, Greg. You've a very serious, penetrating stare. Suspicious, even.'

Greg had laughed.

'Funny you should say that. I nearly did join the police force once. But then . . .' He shrugged. 'I don't know. Maybe it was the danger in the fire service that appealed to my sense of adventure. And in a way, there's a bit of both in the fire service – danger and police work. I mean, sometimes fires are suspicious and we have to try to find out what and who caused them. And of course, I've a lot of friends in the force.'

He had a head of dark, thick but straight hair that she was finding difficult to paint. His pubic hair was, in comparison, a mass of black curls but was proving equally difficult. She never had been good at drawing or painting hair.

Tommy, on the other hand, with a few bold, sweeping strokes, could bring hair so much to life on the canvas that you kept thinking that if you touched it, you'd experience its soft warmth. Tommy was brilliant. One day he was going to be famous and appreciated not only all over Scotland, but all over the world. After all, that's what happened to Charles Rennie Mackintosh, who designed this very building in which they were working.

She'd told Tommy that and he'd said, 'Not if Simon Price can prevent it. He's always making such a fool of my work. I'm beginning to wonder about it myself.'

'Tommy!' Sandra had almost shouted at him. 'You must not let that man make you lose confidence in your talent. Please don't let him win, Tommy. He's as mad as a hatter. Don't let him get to you.'

He'd taken her in his arms and kissed her then.

'Thank God I've got you, Sandra.'

She glanced over at him now, remembering his kiss, and thanked God she'd got him. Not only had he enormous talent, but he was good-looking too, with his fair spiky hair, amber eyes and lean face and figure.

It would be wicked if Simon Price succeeded in undermining Tommy's confidence in himself and his talent. She'd once actually gone to the Director and complained about Price's bullying methods. The Director gave her short shrift. He dismissed her with a flick of his hand and the words, 'The lot of you are darned lucky to get the chance of being taught by such a brilliant artist . . .'

That was surely no excuse for bullying. Of course, Simon Price could be charming to the people at the top. Sandra had often seen him laughing and talking to one director or another. These top guys had no idea how Price treated his students at the lower rungs of the ladder. Especially how he treated Tommy.

'And how's the Pratt doing today?' he was saying now, and staring down at Tommy's canvas. 'Added a couple of strokes since yesterday, I see. Hasn't made much difference, has it? Are you meaning to paint the man or sit there every day just staring at him? Are you sure you weren't meant to be a house painter?'

Sandra watched Price move on to the next student. Her mouth twisted at the sight of his shaved bullet head and gold earring. No doubt he thought he looked young and arty, whereas everyone else thought him old and disgusting. Shaving his head and wearing the same kind of gear as the students didn't change what he was – an ignorant old bully. They all hated him. It wasn't just her.

Tommy, the very one who had reason to hate him most, was the only one who made excuses for him. He'd say things like, 'He's a very talented artist. You only need to look at some of his work.' Or, 'If anyone should know if I've got any talent or not, it's surely him. He must know what he's talking about.'

All the other students groaned at Tommy when they heard him talk like this and tried their best to reassure him. It was so obvious he had talent. He was the most brilliantly talented student among them. One of them said, 'That bastard just wants us all to be clones of him and his so-called Glasgow style.'

Later today, they'd all gather in the lecture theatre and have to listen to Simon Price give a talk. That wasn't so bad, actually. They felt they learned something that way. You could tell then that he knew what he was talking about, as he strolled like a bantam cock, his hands stabbing and circling as he made his points. You could actually feel his enthusiasm and it took the students with him. If only he didn't sneer and wasn't so cruel in his personal criticism when he came round looking at individual students' work. But that was just his horrible nature. He was a bully.

Sandra kept trying to persuade Tommy to ignore him. 'Don't pay any attention to anything he says about your work, Tommy. The more bullies like him get away with it, the worse they get. He picks on you more than the rest of us because he sees he's successful with you. He enjoys upsetting you, Tommy. Don't let him. Raise an eyebrow and stare cheekily back at him like I do.'

But she couldn't see Tommy doing that. He was too anxious to be a good artist. He was far more serious about his work than any of the other students. And he genuinely admired Simon Price's work. She often secretly imagined the pleasure it would be to tear a knife across one of Simon Price's precious paintings. That would teach him.

# 3

Johnny could hardly believe his luck. He was in seventh heaven of happiness as he followed Paul and Renee along the close and up the immaculate stairs, the large stained-glass window on the first landing splashing patches of rainbow colour across the steps. He felt he had really scored at last; he knew good times were ahead.

'Cool! Love your hall – it's stunning.' The hall stretched out in front of him, the doors separated by large panels behind which lights glowed, giving a subtle ambient light. The blond wood flooring reflected the light and enhanced the feeling of spaciousness. At the end of the hall, a large bold abstract painting dominated, basking in the glow of twin spotlights.

Renee led the way towards the first door. 'This is the lounge.'

'Gosh, it's really beautiful.' Johnny gazed in delight at the big windows looking out on to Byres Road. They were topped with a royal-blue pelmet edged with gold, and draped with royal-blue velvet curtains. The ceiling was high with ornate cornicing and a crystal chandelier hung from the centre. The carpet was luxuriously thick and the soft easy chairs looked invitingly comfortable. He couldn't resist sitting down on one of them, and then bouncing up and down on it like a child.

Paul and Renee laughed.

'Come on. It's important you have a good scout around the kitchen. That's where, hopefully, you'll be making a delicious meal for us every night when we come home from the casino.'

'Don't you worry,' Johnny assured them. 'When I was recovering from an illness and was at home a lot with my mother, she taught me some great recipes. I got a lot of experience and practice at cooking then. I'll make you delicious meals, all right. That's a promise.'

'Great.'

He discovered that his mother's kitchen was nothing compared with the ultra-modern kitchen he was now shown. It had every modern convenience imaginable. The original room had obviously been totally remodelled, blond wood units contrasting with stainless steel and slate. The free-standing cooker unit was boldly placed in the centre of the floor, with a stainless steel extractor sweeping up to the ceiling above.

'I can hardly wait to tell Mum about this.'

The flat also had a large bathroom and two double bedrooms. Johnny was intrigued by the built-in wardrobes. One whole wall was made of mirrors and at the touch of a button, the mirrors slid open to reveal a bar holding clothes on hangers and stacks of shelves, some for neatly folded underwear and tops, others for shoes.

Back in the hall, Paul said, 'You understand the main reason we're employing you here, Johnny? And so late at night?'

'Yes, to look after the place while you're at work and have a meal ready when you come home.'

'Yes, but also just to have a presence here in the evenings, with us being out late so regularly. The main thing is to guard the flat against potential burglars. There's been a lot of flats broken into in this area. Some people have been attacked as well, so just to make you feel safer – just for your own protection, we're leaving you this.'

He went over to an oak chest of drawers. 'I expect you to be discreet about this.' From a top drawer, he pulled out a gun. It was a small automatic that sat snugly in the palm of his hand, its leaden sheen giving an aura of power and menace.

Johnny gasped with surprise. His eyes widened with excitement. This was real James Bond stuff. And suddenly Paul appeared just like James Bond. A black-haired James Bond. Suave, handsome and with an equally glamorous lifestyle. Paul returned the gun to the drawer, and Johnny determined that the first time he was alone in the flat, he would hold the gun and do a James Bond act with it, holding it out, swinging it about, aiming it at innumerable criminal intruders. He could hardly wait.

Then Paul and Renee invited him to come with them to visit the casino. He could have danced with joy. His life had taken such a wonderful turn for the better. He wanted to shout about it from the rooftops. Tell everybody. But Paul and Renee asked him to be discreet. It was important to them, they explained, that their private life remained private. And, of course, they had a special image to keep up at the casino.

He longed to tell everything about his new job to all his friends, especially about the gun. However, he didn't want to take the slightest risk of losing such a marvellous job and so he kept quiet.

Johnny followed Paul into the foyer. There was a steward on the door and Paul nodded amiably to him as he strolled over to the reception, where he had to sign Johnny in. Johnny felt a frisson of excitement as the camera took his picture for future reference and for his card. The security door was buzzed open for them and they strode into the gaming area.

'Feel free to have a wander round, Johnny. If you want a drink at the bar, just tell them you're my guest. We'll have something to eat in the restaurant on the balcony later on.'

Johnny looked round in fascination. On both sides were

banks of screens displaying the various games on offer. He was surprised and amused to realise that you could play roulette on a touch screen without ever having to go over to the tables.

He walked over to the cluster of tables where attractive girls in blue dresses controlled the games of roulette and various card games, gamblers carefully studying their cards before moving the chips to complete their bets.

There was an air of suppressed tension and excitement and Johnny wallowed in it.

He slowly walked up the double staircase, drink in hand, to get an overview. He leaned nonchalantly against the banister, the large framed photos of river boats and southern worthies behind him. He stood, arms braced on the rail, surveying the room, drinking in its buzz. He felt important and confident. He continued on to the restaurant area and stared, entranced by the view. Behind the diners was a wall of windows overlooking the river.

It may well have been fairly prosaic in daylight, but it was transformed by the glowing neon lights of the city into a sparkling splash of vibrant colour, reflecting off the smooth waters of the river.

Johnny was to start the next day and Renee gave him money to stock up the fridge and freezer with food from Marks and Spencer's – nothing but the best. And he was to take a taxi back so that he wouldn't need to be carrying anything. He went into town early, and on the way he stopped off at Royal Exchange Square in the hope of seeing some of his friends there. Sure enough, at the back of the Gallery of Modern Art and on the flight of stairs between the pillars at the back of Borders bookshop, he found some of his friends. He loafed about with them for a while, draped back on the steps sharing a spliff with them. He longed to talk about his job but managed to contain himself. It was like a dream and it wasn't the smoke that was causing it. It was real. The glamorous James Bond double, the gorgeous girlfriend. The exciting casino. The beautiful flat. The gun.

He told himself that his friends wouldn't believe him. That made it easier to keep quiet. For now at least. He doubted he could keep such an exciting adventure to himself for ever. After leaving Royal Exchange Square, he walked up to Sauchiehall Street Marks and Spencer's and enjoyed filling the wire trolley from a list he'd already made out. His head was buzzing with ideas for all the meals he planned to cook. He blessed all the hours, indeed years, of his mother's teaching, when he'd been confined to the house. He had never been sure whether she was coaching him to be able to feed himself and look after himself after she was gone, or encourage him to have some sort of talent for a job once he was fit enough to work. Well, it had done that all right. She had probably imagined him eventually baking scones and cakes in some little tearoom, but this, oh, this was so much better than anything he or his mother could ever have imagined. He was getting paid for it as well. Not a big wage, it had to be admitted, but so what! It was still a job in a million, and it suited him perfectly. It didn't entail any heavy work or a boss standing over him harassing him all the time.

Once back in the flat, he packed the food into the fridge and freezer, only leaving out what he'd need for the first evening meal. He had decided on broccoli soup, followed by smoked salmon and cream cheese en croute with a few buttered potatoes and parsley sauce. For dessert, he'd have rice pudding and stewed apples. Then coffee and mints to finish.

Eventually, the table set and everything cooked and ready, and with time to spare before Paul and Renee arrived, he went into the hall, took the gun from the drawer and held it with both hands, arms stretched out in front of him. He pointed it around rapidly, to each side, then he swung right round and aimed down the opposite end of the hall. With each stance, he admired himself in the hall mirror. He thought he looked the part, really tough, ready for anything. No one would dare to enter that door.

As it was, he got quite a shock when he heard a key in the door and realised it was Paul and Renee. Flustered and embarrassed, he flung the gun back into the drawer, slamming it closed as the door swung open. He struggled to look nonchalant.

'Hey there, Johnny. Everything OK?' Paul asked.

'Yes, everything's ready. I'll just go and dish up.'

'No.' Renee put up a protesting hand. 'You don't need to stay and serve us. I can do that. Just show me what you've prepared. We like to relax on our own in the evening. And sometimes you'll just have to leave everything ready because we'll be working into the early hours.'

'I don't mind waiting.'

'No, you just go home to bed.'

Reluctantly, he led her into the kitchen and explained about each course.

'It looks delicious,' Renee said. 'Now off you go.'

Paul was still in the hall, but he'd taken off his smart camel coat. He put out a hand and shook Johnny's.

'It smells delicious, Johnny.'

He opened the door and ushered Johnny out. Clattering triumphantly down the stairs and out on to the still busy Byres Road, Johnny didn't hear Paul and Renee laughing.

Later, as they drove to the casino in their BMW Series 3, they could hardly believe their luck. Johnny was what they had been looking for, exactly what they needed for the success of the plan they'd been nursing for some time. The gun had clinched the deal of working at the flat, of course. It made Johnny immediately imagine he was some sort of courageous hero.

They reached the casino and sat for a few minutes savouring how successful their plan was going to be and how it would change their lives. Rain sparkled down the windscreen, jewels of light caught in the neon reflection of the casino.

'There's still one thing I can't help worrying about,' Renee said eventually. 'OK, he's a naive idiot, but will he have enough nerve to go along with the plan? After all, it's a risky robbery.'

'What's risky about it?'

Renee laughed. 'For God's sake, Paul. We're talking a fortune here.'

'But it's perfect. We've got a copy of the key to the safe. We know the manager looks forward to his night break in the staff dining room and he leaves his office on the dot at the same time every night. We know he sits and reads his book while he eats his two rolls and bacon and drinks two cups of coffee. He's there for nearly an hour every night, concentrating on his book and chewing at his dentures. He's been doing it for years. We've been watching him for years, haven't we? He's never once deviated from his routine.' Paul grinned. 'It gives Johnny plenty of time to nip in the side window and empty the safe of all that lovely cash that's waiting to be put in the bank first thing in the morning.'

'I know all that. All I'm saying is, will Johnny muster enough nerve to do it?'

'Well, there's the motivation first of all. We'll tell him what a perfect life he could give his mother and sister with his share of the money, and how they'll be able to start a wonderful new life abroad, and so on.'

'What if that still doesn't give him enough nerve?'

'For God's sake, you worry too much. We can tell him to take the gun. Not to use it. There'll be no need for that. Only to make him feel more confident, a big James Bond hero. Just leave Johnny to me, OK?'

They entered the casino and, as they worked at their tables, they kept glancing over to the door of the manager's office, past the tense faces of the gamblers. Dead on time, the door opened and the manager, in his smart black suit and black bow tie, appeared. As usual, he was clutching his book. He was a thin, lanky guy with a long, pinched nose. The only time he wore spectacles was when he was reading his book. They perched on the end of his nose and any croupiers who saw him said they were surprised his specs didn't slip off his nose and splash into his coffee.

After three-quarters of an hour, the tall figure appeared again, walked back to the office and shut the door behind him. Johnny would have plenty of time to get in, open the safe and stuff all the money into the bag that Renee had made especially for the purpose. It was to be fastened round his chest, under his coat. Then he would escape back through the window and return to his house in Botanic Crescent. That way, there would be no connection between the robbery and any of the croupiers. Later, when they thought it to be safe, they would collect the money from Johnny. Admittedly, they would have a lot of persuading to do to get Johnny to go along with the plan, but they were becoming more and more certain that they could do it.

# 4

They used to call Hamish Ferguson 'Fatty Ferguson' when he was at secondary school. They ignored his pimples. That, he supposed, was because quite a few of the other pupils, boys and girls alike, suffered the same disadvantage. Bad skin seemed to be just another problem of being a teenager. However, Hamish was the only overweight pupil in the class at secondary school and he was never allowed to forget it.

At home, his mother was ashamed of him. At least, she never wanted to be seen with him. She was very glamorous for an older woman. She did her best to look younger. She'd had what she called 'a boob job'. She'd had her long hair dyed blond and it was hooked back and up with a frilly elastic band, and she wore embarrassingly short denim skirts. She certainly could attract men – younger men especially. If she had a boyfriend in the house, Hamish had to hide himself in his room. Or, more often, he had to get out and wander the streets. Or he'd hang around in cafés until the coast was clear. Sometimes he'd go to the pictures. His mother was never mean with money. From when he was quite young, he would sit for ages in McDonald's or places like that, eating burgers and chips. Lots of ice cream too, of course. Looking back now, he supposed that was why he'd put on so much weight and was nicknamed Fatty.

Thank goodness it was different at the Glasgow School of Art. Nobody called him anything but Hamish there. There were about twenty students in the Life class and all were busy, like him, studying the model and concentrating on trying to transfer a good likeness of him or her on to their canvases.

At break time, they'd all go across the road to the rec. There they could get some fruit and even veggie stuff at lunchtime. Quite often now, he'd try the veggie stuff and already he had lost quite a bit of weight. Even his skin, although far from perfect, had begun to show signs of clearing up.

He tried to hang on to the company of the other art students for as long as possible. Often he went with them to one of the pubs or clubs after the day at the Art School finished. He'd started to put gel on his hair like the other blokes. Unlike some of the others, though, he kept his hair short and so just had small spikes. Some of the others had really showy shapes. He didn't want too much attention paid to his plump face. Although maybe it would have been better to have high Mohican-style spikes. Maybe that way, more attention would have been drawn to his hair instead of to his face. It was a big problem.

Now his mother had another boyfriend. She said he was special. He was different, and he wanted to move in with her. He was different, all right. Usually her boyfriends were quite a few years younger than her. This one – his name was Damon, of all things – looked not much older than Hamish. In fact, now that he came to think of it, he remembered a Damon in the last year of secondary school when he'd started in his first year. He'd never actually met the guy but he'd heard the name bandied about and made fun of. It could have been the same person. If it was the same Damon, that meant he would only be a few years older than Hamish. He would still be in his twenties. It was ridiculous. Hamish had blurted that out to his mother and she was furious.

'If you don't like it, you know what you can do. Get out. I'm sick of you criticising my friends.'

'I never say a word about your friends,' Hamish protested.

'Yes you do. And Damon is more than a friend. He's moving in and I'm not having you making both our lives miserable. You'll have to get out. And I mean to digs. Any place except here.'

Hamish was completely flummoxed by this. He'd never been allowed to be seen by her men before, but he'd never dreamt she would go this far. Not his mother. Sometimes, right enough, he wondered if she really was his mother. Maybe he'd been adopted at birth or something. Maybe she'd just been looking after him for somebody else. But, come to think of it, she had never looked after him. He'd lost count of the number of babysitters he'd had when he was young. He'd never known his father, and his mother had kept moving around and changing her job. Hamish's younger days had been a terrible mix-up of people and places. Some of the babysitters had been the pits. He tried not to remember them. His mother never seemed to care what they were like.

But actually putting him out, abandoning him completely?

'But . . . but where will I go?'

'You heard me – into digs. Lots of students live in digs. Why shouldn't you?'

'But I've no money.'

'I'll pay your digs for the first week. I'm always giving you money as it is. You eat like a bloody horse. It'll be worth it to get rid of you. I want you out of here tomorrow, whether you've found digs or not. Do you hear?'

He felt so shattered, he could have started blubbering right there and then. Only with a supreme effort, and a very deep breath, did he prevent the tears from escaping. He even managed a strong and casual-sounding 'OK'.

Next day, during the first break, he'd told some of the lads that he was looking for digs. Mike Jones gave him the name of a landlady who might have a room to let. Mike had met someone in the pub who was living there but he was going down south to work and so would be leaving the area.

Hamish went immediately after the class finished to the address Mike had given him. It was quite near the fire station, a run-down looking tenement, blackened with age. He went into the close. It stank of cat pee. He tried to find the name plate of Mrs McCormick. He found it on the top floor and knocked on the door. It was opened by a sour-faced elderly woman. She looked about ninety.

'Hello.' Hamish smiled nervously at her. 'I believe you have a room to let. I'm a student at the Glasgow School of Art and one of the other students heard you might be looking for a lodger.'

'Come in.' She stood aside. 'What's your name?'

'Hamish. Hamish Ferguson.'

He followed her through a dark lobby into a shabby sitting room.

'Sit down.'

He sat down.

'I'm not looking for anybody.'

'Oh, I'm sorry . . .' He made to rise again.

'But now that you're here,' she said, 'you might as well stay.'

She then proceeded to list the rules of the house and the rent she charged.

'I don't like anyone in my kitchen, so you'll have to eat out.'

'That's OK. I'm used to eating out.'

'No smoking in the house.'

'That's OK. I don't smoke.'

'No drugs in the house.'

'That's OK. I don't do drugs.'

'No drink in the house.'

'That's OK as well.'

He was already depressed and bored with the whole idea. It sounded as if he would be even worse off than he had been with his mother. But he couldn't stay at home and so this would have to do until he found a better place.

'Well? It's vacant.'

'Can I move in tonight then?'

'A week's rent in advance.'

'OK, I'll pay you as soon as I come back with my things.'

He had left his bag in the shop at the Art School. The School stayed open later for guided tours. People came from all over the world to see the Charles Rennie Mackintosh building and all his other work.

Hamish tried to smile and sound cheerful, as if he was looking forward to coming back. He failed, and Mrs McCormick got up and shuffled towards the sitting-room door.

'I suppose I'd better show you the room.'

Hamish had never heard such a sour and grudging voice.

It was a big flat with several doors leading off the lobby. She pushed open a door which led into a room covered with dark brown varnished paper. In the room was a big double bed, a huge wardrobe, an ancient chest of drawers, a bedside table and two wooden chairs. There were no ornaments anywhere, not even a single picture on the wall. For a second, Hamish thought of hanging one of his paintings to cheer the place up. But only for a second. Mrs McCormick, he suspected, was far too miserable to allow that, and would immediately order him out, especially if she saw a painting of a nude figure. There hadn't been any pictures or ornaments of any kind in the sitting room either.

'That's the room.'

'OK. Fine,' he lied. He'd never seen any house so ghastly and depressing, and he'd seen more than a few in his day. His mother had dragged him around innumerable houses of all sizes and types, in town and country areas.

Thinking of his mother, he could imagine her at this very moment giggling and flirting like a young thing with her latest man. Happy as a lark, she'd be, and never giving her son a thought. There was something far wrong with her. Or was it him? Maybe it was something wrong with him. He wouldn't be a bit surprised. As he returned down the dark stairway, he was taking deep breaths again, fighting to prevent himself drowning in a storm of tears.

# 5

Twice they'd been out now. Only in the afternoon, which happened to suit Greg's shift. He'd called at the house for her and she'd asked him in to meet her mother. Her mother had insisted that she and Greg go out for the afternoon and assured them both that she would be fine on her own.

'She fusses far too much over me,' she told Greg. 'I had a bit of mild angina some months ago but I'm really perfectly all right now. And Kirsty needs to get out more.'

Johnny had appeared then, but he was on his way out. He was going down to Paul and Renee's flat, he explained, and would be there until late that evening, or the early hours of the morning. This had become his routine. They were all usually in bed by the time he returned.

Kirsty had told Greg about the job and about Paul and Renee, and Greg thought it seemed strange as well.

'I'm not surprised you're worried,' he said. 'All the same, he's a grown man, Kirsty. It's up to him now what company he keeps and what he does with his life.'

They had gone to a film matinee at the Glasgow Film Theatre and sat in the back row. That first time Greg had put his arm around her, the colours of the film flickering over his face as he leaned close, his arm enveloping her. She sat enthralled in the darkness of the cinema, with the feel of his warm breath on her hair. She had never before in her life felt so happy. On the second date, he had nuzzled his lips into her neck. Then he'd kissed her on the mouth, gently at first, and then with growing passion, and she had responded with equal passion. It wasn't until afterwards, when she learned Greg's shift was changing and he expected her to go out with him in the evening, that she began to worry again.

He hadn't actually met her father, not to speak to. But in the Art School, where he'd been doing a bit of modelling to make some extra cash, he'd seen her father and heard the way he spoke to the students. Loyalty to her, she supposed, stopped him from voicing any criticism. He was impressed, though, by her father's talent as a painter. Everybody admired her father for that.

She hesitated when Greg asked her to come out at night.

'Why not?' he wanted to know. 'You heard what your mother said. You'll be telling me next that you have to stay in to feed the cat.'

She managed a smile. 'All right.'

Greg looked delighted. 'I'll call for you at eight o'clock. OK?'

She nodded, and for the rest of the day she tried to reassure herself that there was nothing her father could do. Greg was too strong a character. He wouldn't stand for any nonsense from her father. On her part, she was too much in love to listen to anything her father might say and do in an attempt to undermine or spoil her relationship with Greg. So everything would be all right.

She was still surprised, though, when Greg called for her and she introduced him to her father.

'Ah!' Her father had been overflowing with bonhomie. 'You're the model, best one we've ever had. A firefighter as well. Salt of the earth!'

She was waiting for him to add, 'What the hell does a man like you see in her?'

But he didn't. Not in front of Greg, at least. He kept that, and other scathing remarks, for later, after she returned and was alone.

She didn't let him get to her. Not this time. Not that she'd ever got as upset as Johnny always did. For one thing, she never tried to please her father. Poor Johnny was always struggling to please him and never succeeding.

She had enjoyed the evening with Greg so much that it had seemed too good to be true, but she didn't believe she was just another conquest for him. He seemed genuinely fond of her. Concerned about her, too.

'I always know,' he said, 'when that brother of yours has been up to something. After he's been in, you're always left anxious and worried.'

'He's not been up to anything, Greg. It's just he's a bit naive and easily influenced. His friends became Goths, for instance, and so he became one too.'

'He seems a bit old for that caper. The ones I've seen hanging around at the back of Borders bookshop look more like daft teenagers.'

'I know. It's just as I say – he's a bit immature for his age. But I don't think he and his friends do anything wrong, I mean against the law. At least, I hope not.'

'Well, stop worrying then.'

'But I can't help worrying about that pair he works for.'

'They're not Goths, are they?'

'Oh no. Paul wears a black T-shirt and trousers at work. That's what the men there all wear, apparently, and the women wear blue. When they're not at work, though, both look very smart. Off duty, Renee wears designer-label dresses and her hair piled up. Talk about glamorous. And I'm sure they'll both be in their thirties at least.'

'OK, that's a bit odd as well. A couple like that teaming up with your Goth-type young brother, but it may be just as they said. They need somebody to look after their place. There have been a lot of burglaries, right enough.'

She didn't tell him that the latest thing was they'd told Johnny they'd leave a gun in the drawer of the hall table for his protection, in case the flat was broken into. Johnny had been thrilled and excited.

'A real gun, Kirsty. I held it, and pointed it at myself in the mirror, and kidded on I was John Wayne.'

'Are you mad, Johnny? Please don't touch the gun ever again. Even if it's legal, it's a very bad idea.'

He laughed, enjoying himself and obviously not seeing the danger or the probable illegality of having access to such a weapon. The more she thought of the gun and Johnny having his hands on it, the more her blood froze with fear. She tried to put him off it. She tried to persuade him to tell Paul and Renee to remove it from the house. What did they want him to do with it anyway? Shoot and kill an intruder? For that, Johnny might be arrested for murder.

But Johnny was too happy and excited to pay any attention to her. Every day, he left for the flat, whistling cheerfully to himself, sometimes even doing a little dance every now and then as he went along the road.

Kirsty despaired of him. Every time she tried to talk to him and express her worries, all he did was laugh at her, and tell her she was the best sister in the world and he loved her. He'd always been such a demonstrative and affectionate person, even as a young child. He was so loving, it was impossible for anyone not to love him in return. Except for her father, of course. He didn't seem capable of loving anybody except himself. He would only make everything a thousand times worse if Johnny got into any trouble.

But maybe it was as Greg said – they just needed somebody

to look after their place because there had been so many burglaries.

Suddenly Kirsty jerked with fright. But all that had startled her was Jingles, the cat, jumping onto her lap. She stroked it, thinking to herself that she was being ridiculous worrying herself into such a state over Johnny.

It was true what Greg said. Johnny was a grown man and it was up to him what company he kept and what he did with his life. She tried to practise deep breathing to calm herself. Yes, it was definitely true what Greg said.

She tried not to think about the gun.

# 6

Hamish had gone back to ask his mother for the money she had promised him. She didn't allow him in, barred him from entering, standing at the door. It was the final insult. She called back into the house, 'It's just the paper boy come for his money, darling. I won't be a minute.' Her voice dropped to a hiss. 'Wait there. Don't move.' She returned and stuffed a few notes into his hand. 'Get a bloody job.' Then she shut the door in his face.

He counted the notes, blinking as he did. He'd have to get a job all right. He supposed he'd been lucky up till now. Most of the other students already had part-time weekend and evening jobs. His mother had never bothered to charge him for rent and food. So at least she had been generous. Maybe too much so. He suddenly thought, 'I've been lazy – a fat, lazy slob.' He'd better do something about that right away, otherwise he wouldn't have enough money for food or rent.

So before even going to the Art School to collect his bag, he went into a supermarket along Great Western Road which had advertised part-time vacancies for evening shelf-stackers. He asked if he could see the manager, and after a five-minute wait, he was ushered into the manager's office at the back. He was asked briefly about his availability for shifts, and also about his interests and course at the Art School, before the manager said that he would be taken on. He was to start the following evening. That cheered him up a bit. He then went to collect his bag. It contained a change of clothes and shoes, a few books, some paints, brushes and a sketch pad, and a few toiletries. The girls in the shop had made no objection to looking after the bag. He was used to being ignored and they barely even interrupted their conversation with each other while one of them handed over the bag. From there, he made his way back to the digs, his spurt of cheerfulness and gratitude frittering out. The gloom of the tenement entrance and stairway and the silent upstairs flat enfolded him in black depression and hopelessness. He tried to concentrate his thoughts on the Art School. He really enjoyed it and the painting he did there. He was lucky to be able to go every day. The tutors were excellent and very helpful. Simon Price could be a bit nasty and aggressive, but helpful nevertheless. Mr Daiches was an elderly gay gentleman, rather flamboyant with his slightly Edwardian look, his high-buttoned suit jacket with matching waistcoat and silk handkerchief overflowing from his top pocket. He had occasionally tried to make a pass at one of the male students. He was invariably repulsed. The blokes were all into pretty girls, not old poofters. But Mr Daiches never took offence. He was a nice old bloke, really, and a very good tutor.

Hamish didn't sleep very well that night. He felt lost and alone in the big double bed, which was strange because, after all, he had always slept alone. The room was stuffy and the bedclothes heavy. He got up twice to open the window. It wouldn't budge. He jerked and strained at it until eventually, defeated, he leaned his forehead against the glass for a few seconds before returning to bed.

The next day, he took the bus into Sauchiehall Street and bought a sandwich in a newsagent's. He munched at it as he climbed the hill to the Art School. The newsagent's had a few postcards in its window, some advertising various articles for sale. There was only one place advertised to let, but it was a flat with a rent of a hundred and fifty pounds a week. That was out of his league. There were other shop windows in other streets, though. And there were agencies. He would try them all. He had to try because Mrs McCormick's place was the pits.

Once in the art class, he smiled and gave the others a nod of friendly greeting. He wondered what sort of accommodation they had. Some of them still lived at home with their parents, of course. Most of them no doubt paid rent to their mothers from money earned at part-time jobs. Only Betty Powell didn't seem to have a job and she lived at home, he'd heard someone say. He should have paid his mother rent long ago. He felt guilty about that now.

As usual, he listened more than talked during the breaks. Today it was more because he felt exhausted with lack of sleep, but there had always been a quiet, shy side to him. He dreaded spending another night at Mrs McCormick's, but before that he had to work for several hours in the supermarket. He managed the shelf-stacking all right, but he had also to lift heavy boxes to and fro and that really drained away any energy he had left. He managed to get a cup of tea in the staff canteen, which helped him a bit. He was intensely relieved, however, when it was time for him to leave. He decided to take a short cut through the Botanic Gardens and he hadn't gone very far when he saw Mr Daiches, looking flamboyant as usual, with a black fedora rakishly poised on his head.

'Hello, my boy,' the old man greeted him. 'Have you been at the orchestra concert in the Kibble Palace?'

'No, I've been working in the supermarket along the road. I'm just taking a short cut back to my digs.'

Mr Daiches sighed. 'What a wonderful experience you missed. An absolutely wonderful performance of the divine Mozart. His operas are my favourite. Are you familiar with his operas? *The Magic Flute*, *Don Giovanni*, *The Marriage of Figaro*?'

Hamish shook his head.

'Forgive me, my boy, but what is your name? I've become somewhat forgetful recently. Old age, you know.'

'Hamish Ferguson, sir. I've been to some of your lectures.' He hesitated, then added, 'I liked your take on Hockney's paintings. I really feel more in tune with him now.'

'Why, thank you, Hamish. Very good of you, I'm sure.'

For a few minutes they walked together in silence, until suddenly they were surprised by a whey-faced youth with a hooded top and white tracksuit bottoms tucked into his football socks.

'Hey pal,' he greeted them, 'ye got a smoke?'

'Sorry, I don't,' Hamish responded, and he and Mr Daiches continued their walk.

They were approaching the side gate when suddenly they were surrounded by five youths, one of whom was the 'hoodie' who had spoken to them before.

'Whit's yer problem, eh? Why did ye no' gie us a smoke, eh? Whit's yer problem? Are we no' good enough or what?'

Hamish shook his head.

'Sorry, I don't understand. What do you mean? I don't smoke, that was all.'

'I only smoke cigars,' Mr Daiches said. 'You may have one if you wish. They are quite a good brand. I always say . . .'

'Aw, shut up, ye stupid auld poofter.' And with that, the ned thrust forward and rammed his head into the bridge of Mr Daiches's nose. Mr Daiches staggered back with a cry of pain. Hamish tried to get in front of the old man to protect him from further violence, only to suffer a similar blow himself. A blinding pain shot through him, and involuntarily tears welled in his eyes with the shock. He too staggered back, and before he knew what to do next, the other neds all started swinging punches and kicks at both him and Mr Daiches. They both frantically tried to ward them off, but were soon knocked to the ground. They curled into a ball, hands round heads, as their attackers continued violently kicking them, shouting – and worst of all laughing – as they booted the defenceless pair. At last, tired of the assault and breathing heavily, the neds stopped and as they strolled away grinning, one of them called back, 'We fair smoked you, ye pair o' fags.'

Hamish eventually managed to crawl to his feet. Then he helped Mr Daiches, but the old man only managed to get to his knees.

'I'm sorry, my boy. You'll have to take my mobile phone from my pocket and get a taxi for me. For us both. I feel very weak and dizzy.'

Hamish could see blood pouring down Mr Daiches's face. Blood was pouring down the side of his own face. He could feel it seeping into his T-shirt. He managed to find Mr Daiches's phone and called for a taxi to take them both to the Royal Infirmary. He felt enraged and frustrated, and it wasn't just the physical pain of the beating. It was the sheer hopelessness and humiliation that hurt him the most.

# 7

Glasgow's first Royal Infirmary was designed by the world-famous architects James and Robert Adam. As the population of the city grew, a larger building was needed. One third of all patients died after the simplest operations. Many died of cholera and were buried in mass graves. Additions to the original Royal Infirmary were built on top of these mass graves. This went on until Joseph Lister recognised the need for sterile conditions.

A new infirmary was built after the original Adam building and the Lister wing had been pulled down. This was much criticised at the time because, for one thing, it was on the west side of the cathedral and would completely dwarf it. However, the project went ahead and its grim and bulky proportions made it the largest building in the United Kingdom at the time. The infirmary had always been funded by voluntary contributions and one of the best known of these voluntary sources was the money collected each year by the city's students through the streets of Glasgow. It seemed incredible now that places like the Royal Infirmary and everywhere that people needed medical or surgical treatment were dependent on voluntary contributions, much of it raised by the conscientious efforts of university students.

Hamish was certainly glad of the National Health Service now that he urgently needed help.

The taxi pulled into the small drop-off lay-by outside the massive square building that housed the Accident and Emergency department. Groaning, they clambered stiffly out and staggered through the group of smokers who had collected at the entrance.

Inside, there was a waiting area and a counter with a frosted glass window where people had to report on arrival. There was already a police presence, although it was early evening. The admissions were dealt with behind heavy toughened glass screens, and drunks milled about in the waiting area, loudly talking and arguing. Minor scuffles would occasionally break out, but were quickly suppressed by the security guards. Hamish and Mr Daiches sat quietly in a corner, trying to remain inconspicuous. Hamish found it incredible that such violence could be going on in a hospital waiting room. The language was loud and foul as well. Hamish was very sorry indeed for the nurses and doctors who had to deal constantly with such people.

After they had seen a doctor and a nurse and were patched up, they nervously emerged from the hospital and into the taxi they had called. Hamish once again blessed Mr Daiches's mobile phone.

'I would be most obliged, dear boy, if you would see me safely home and into my bed. I fear I am not able to alight from this taxi cab without your help and support.'

'OK.'

Mr Daiches lived quite near the Glasgow Art Gallery and Museum. A cluster of spires and towers topped the huge red sandstone building. It was one of Hamish's favourite places. Many an hour he'd spent there. Apart from a magnificent collection of paintings by the great Dutch and Renaissance masters, there was a wonderful range of Impressionist works.

Some of the best examples of Rembrandt, Botticelli, Monet and Picasso could be admired on the walls of its halls and picture promenade gallery.

There were also examples of Charles Rennie Mackintosh's paintings and furniture.

'Take the necessary payment from my wallet, dear boy,' Mr Daiches said when they arrived at their destination.

Hamish paid the driver and then half-carried Mr Daiches into his flat. He tried not to groan with the intense pain he himself was suffering. He was truly thankful that it was a ground-floor flat and there were no stairs to climb.

Mr Daiches fumbled for his key chain and opened the door. As they both hobbled inside and shut the door behind them, Mr Daiches said, 'Dear boy, dare I ask you yet another favour?'

'Sure.'

'A cup of tea would be so very welcome.'

'Where's the kitchen?'

'Just at the end of the lobby. If I could just have a seat in the front room, over there on the right.'

Hamish helped him into a room with an old-fashioned moquette suite, a piano and a dark red Turkish-style carpet. Hamish lowered Mr Daiches into one of the fireside easy chairs.

'OK?'

'I deeply appreciate your help, dear boy. You are an extremely kind young man.'

Hamish shrugged.

'Milk and sugar?'

'Milk and two sugars, thank you so much. I will never forget your kindness. What is your name, dear boy? Forgive me, have you told me before?'

'Hamish. Hamish Ferguson.'

Hamish left and made his painful way through to the

kitchen to find what was needed to make a pot of tea. In a few minutes he returned carrying two cups.

'I feel I need this myself.'

'Yes, Hamish. It has been a dreadful night for both of us. And to think I had been having such a lovely time at the classical concert.' He took a sip of tea and sighed. 'The divine Mozart. Are you familiar with any of his music?'

Hamish shrugged. 'It's all art with me. And architecture. And history. I like history. Scottish history.'

'Ah yes. Obviously art is my main subject. But next to art, I have a keen appreciation of music. Of course, my mother was a beautiful pianist. She used to take me to concerts even when I was very young. Was it art galleries your mother took you to?'

Hamish started to laugh but had to cut his hilarity short because of the pain in his chest.

'No, my mother never bothered with me. Usually it was babysitters but they never bothered much with me either.'

'Oh, my dear boy.'

Hamish shrugged.

'I just went around on my own. I always found a library or an art gallery wherever we happened to be staying. I'd sit there for a while either admiring the pictures or reading books about art and architecture and Scottish history.' He took a noisy sup from his cup. 'I managed all right.'

Mr Daiches shook his head and sighed and sipped at his tea.

'Where do you live, Hamish?'

'Round from the Queen Margaret Drive fire station.'

'Dear, dear. You can't go away over there in the state you're in. I have a spare bedroom. You are welcome to stay there tonight.'

Hamish hesitated but he certainly did not feel able to make his way to his digs.

'OK.'

Eventually he helped Mr Daiches into his bedroom, but drew the line at helping him to undress. He escaped into the other bedroom and collapsed on to the double bed there, only drawing the big satin quilt over himself.

What a dreadful night, as Mr Daiches had said.

And more to come, Hamish thought, remembering his digs.

# 8

Betty Powell hated to leave the Art School every day and return to her widowed mother's flat in Great Western Road. She was an only child born late in her mother's marriage. Her father had died when she was a baby and so she had no recollection of him. It seemed a miracle that her mother had conceived at all. She had such a disgust of sex and the men who perpetrated the revolting act. Her mother spoke of her father, if she spoke of him at all, as if he had been some sort of predatory animal.

Mrs Powell was always warning her daughter about what animals men were and never to have anything to do with them. She even had a disgust of the human body and all its functions. Betty had never been warned about the onset of menstruation or given any explanation of it. Even sanitary towels had never been mentioned.

Betty could just imagine her mother's horror if she knew about the life drawing and painting classes she was taking and especially how, at the moment, she was painting a nude male model. Her mother thought she was attending an embroidery class. She'd shown her mother a photo of the embroidery studio with its long tables and chairs set out for needlework. And of course, Betty had assured her, it was an all-female class.

Her mother didn't know about her poetry either. If her

mother ever found any of the verses she'd penned, she'd be certain that her daughter was going down to hell to burn there forever. Her powerful sexual feelings overflowed into poetry and vibrated on the page and throbbed to a climax almost like sex itself. Or what she imagined sex would be like. Now the images were becoming even more real and vivid, since she had seen Greg McFarlane's naked body. Every day she sat at her easel and devoured every inch of him. Every day her mind and her body throbbed with sexual passion. Nobody guessed, of course. To all the other students, she was just a mousy-haired, bespectacled girl and a bit of a loner.

How she envied Sandra Matheson and the obvious love affair she was enjoying with Tommy Pratt. At least, she had thought like that until she had seen Greg McFarlane and realised what stronger emotions could be aroused. Sandra, and the other female students, didn't seem at all aroused or even interested in Greg McFarlane, except of course as a model, something to copy on to canvas.

Only the tutor had noticed something that set her heart racing with panic and made a flush burn over her face. He'd said, 'What's happening here? Are you having difficulty with the genital area or what? You seem to have got stuck on that penis.'

'I think I've got it now.' Her voice wavered nervously. 'Haven't I?'

'Seems a bit on the big side to me but if that's how you see it . . .'

Fortunately it was time for their break, which abruptly ended the conversation. The tutor liked his breaks. He usually spent them with one of the directors.

Greg had pulled on a pair of black trousers and a black T-shirt. Apparently, all the firefighters wore black trousers and black T-shirts. He was already chatting with Tommy and Sandra and some of the others, and they were all trooping out to the rec for the lunch break. It seemed amazing to Betty how calm they all were, as if this morning had been just another ordinary day, and Greg McFarlane was just another ordinary man. She was drowning with passion for him as she followed everyone outside, eyes lowered, silent. Her palms were moist with sweat as she fantasised guiltily about various rescue scenarios where Greg would sweep up her naked body and hold it close to him as he burst out of a burning building. Inside of her, a poem was forming like a lifebelt, floating towards her, rescuing her.

I hide behind my thumb
under the guise of the first
lesson in perspective. I stretch
my arm out like a thin, pale promontory
my thumb as beacon,
rigid at the far end
warning of the rocks beyond.

My first life model, on the first day
of Life classes is naked. And male.
Wearing nothing
but an everyday expression.

The statues that line the hall didn't prepare me.
Smooth and cold and lifelike no comparison
for smooth and warm and life. With hair.
I didn't know there would be so much hair.

Dark against the celtic pale of his skin,
it marked him with a t-shape. The crossbar
waved and curled across the tight muscle of his chest
meeting in the middle
where it warmed his heart.

My eye traces the line as it narrows
on its own path to the navel, before
swelling into a dark tattoo at the groin.
The man must have read my line of sight.
His cheeks bunch with a suppressed smile.

Mine burn as bright as a lighthouse.
I withdraw from his scrutiny
And find sanctuary behind my thumb.

When she arrived home later that day, her mother had high tea ready for her as usual, and was fussing about, putting home-made scones on the top of a three-tiered cake stand. Scones on the top plate, a Victoria sponge in the middle, and on the bottom plate, some digestive and rich tea biscuits. It was always the same, stuck in a post-war time warp. Sometimes there was a patterned lace table cover but today, the tea cloth had flowers at each corner, all embroidered by her mother. Her mother liked to sit of an evening doing a bit of embroidery while listening to her radio. She refused to have a television set in the house.

'There's far too much disgusting behaviour on television. I don't know how it's allowed.' She read about it every week in her *Radio Times*, and heard about it from her next-door neighbour. She was also continuously shocked and disgusted by what she regularly saw from her front-room window. Couples walked along with arms around each other's waists and often stopped to kiss one another passionately. There was a café across the road that had metal tables and chairs outside, and more than once she'd seen a youth put his hand up a girl's very short skirt as they sat together, supposedly drinking coffee. Her mother didn't know what the world was coming to.

The radio was in the front room, along with a dark brown,

low-backed, leather, buttoned chesterfield and a davenport. The davenport was a particular type of ladies' writing desk. Betty had found out that its name stemmed from a Captain Davenport, who commissioned the first desk of its type from Gillows of Lancaster. Her mother was very proud of this writing desk and Betty didn't dare tell her about its connection with one of the hated male species.

The fireplace was fronted by a brass table on which was displayed her mother's collection of paperweights. The paperweights were made by hand and so no two were alike. A good piece was unexpectedly heavy and the images within the glass were delicately coloured and beautiful.

'How was your day, Betty?' her mother asked.

'We were all working away as usual. I told you about the long tables we sit at. We often chat while we sew and show each other what we're working on.'

'Very nice. I'm looking forward to seeing your work at the end of your course.'

This didn't bother Betty. She'd already bought a beautiful embroidered wall-hanging she had found in a charity shop in the West End. It had unusual motifs based on Glasgow's history. She had secreted it away in her locker at the Art School, ready to be shown to her mother when the time came.

Her mother poured the tea from an ornate silver teapot. Her father had left them very well provided for, but of course he never even got any credit for that.

'It's a comfort to me to know,' her mother said, 'that you are safely among girls like yourself and there are lady tutors.'

'Yes, it's really very nice, very respectable.'

'Good. I'm glad to hear it.'

The room lapsed into silence as they sipped their tea and delicately cut little portions of lemon sole. Betty was thinking of another poem.

I scratched at the paper with my charcoal
thumbed the black dust into a softer line
ignoring the thump of my heart
and the voice of my mother intoning
like a Bible class in my head.

Are all men casual in nudity like him,
I wondered as he scratched his right buttock
before he settled into the pose?

I allowed my eyes to roam.
Seeing a rhythm of skin and muscle
and hair and contained energy.
A harmony of nature and future.
How to evidence all that
with nothing but dark and light?

An area of white where the light
shone on the sheen of his thigh.
Then a spectrum of grey to highlight
the curve of muscle, the promise of strength.

I forced my hand to move
as I filled in the last space on the page
. . . his maleness bunched at the junction
of his thighs, like an advert for rude health.

I was sure everyone could hear my heart
thicken the pulse to my ears.
And was certain everyone could sense
the forbidden heat and tingle
that shortened my breath.

Afterwards as I stooped at the sink
about to plunge my hands into warm water,
I examined the coal deep
in the whorls of my fingers and thought
if mother was here she would say
the stains on my soul
would not erase so easily.

# 9

They got together as often as they could. They saw each other in the fire station if Greg was on duty in the morning, but their meetings there were always brief, in among a crowd of other firefighters. Or they were interrupted by his duties. If he wasn't called away to deal with a fire or a road accident or any emergencies, he was working with the others in the yard outside the station.

There was the maintenance of the vehicles and equipment to attend to. Then they often had training sessions with other stations so that they could work efficiently together when necessary. Among other things, they had to do fire safety visits, advising people how to protect their premises from fire.

Often there were parties of schoolchildren and others visiting the station and being shown around and advised about how to keep themselves safe. Children especially loved these visits, trying on the helmets and getting a shot at the hose reel.

When Greg was off duty, they met regularly – almost every day. They had grown really close. The only little bits of friction that arose between them were caused by Greg's attitude to Johnny. He didn't have the patience for him that Kirsty had. Of course, he hadn't known Johnny as he was growing up. He hadn't known the lovable child, or the teenager who had suffered agonies with rheumatic fever and never complained, but was always so grateful for anything anybody did to help him.

However, Greg was getting so annoyed at what he thought was Kirsty's totally unnecessary anxiety about Johnny that she eventually told him about the gun.

Greg's annoyance immediately turned to fury.

'The bloody idiot! I bet that pair don't even have a licence for it. I'll talk to him. I'll talk to Paul and Renee as well. If necessary, I'll have word with Jack Campbell.'

'No! No! Please, Greg,' Kirsty pleaded, 'I don't want to spoil everything for him. He's never been able to hold a job for very long with his health problems. This is the first one that really suits him and he's so happy. No, leave it with me. I'll speak to him about the gun.'

She persuaded Greg to simmer down eventually, but she resolved to try to be more careful in future and either not mention Johnny to Greg, or at least appear to be calmer and less anxious.

If it had not been for all the worry about Johnny (and perhaps her worries were needless, she kept trying to tell herself), she would have been blissfully happy. Then Greg proposed, and she couldn't help laughing.

'Darling, we've only been going out together for a few weeks.'

'We've known each other longer than that. Anyway, what does time matter? We love each other and I want you to move in with me as soon as possible.'

'But Tommy shares your flat.'

'I know, but Sandra's really keen for him to move in with her. She's got a flat in Charing Cross Mansions.'

Kirsty still hesitated.

'But . . .'

'Don't you dare make Johnny an excuse for not leaving home.'

'No, I wasn't, but . . .'

'Kirklee Terrace is only a few minutes away from Botanic Crescent,' Greg reminded her, 'and as far as your mother's concerned, she'll be happy for you, I'm sure.'

Kirsty knew this to be true and she secretly suspected that, as usual, Johnny was at the root of her anxiety. That could be the only reason for her hesitation, because she was sure nothing would make her happier than marrying Greg and moving to his lovely converted flat in Kirklee Terrace. It was situated just next to the side entrance to the Botanic Gardens and so had a beautiful view into the gardens from the kitchen window. The front sitting-room window looked down over a grassy slope on to the busy Great Western Road.

She said 'Yes' to Greg's proposal, and just as he predicted, her mother was delighted and immediately launched into plans for the wedding. Her mother had once been a dressmaker and now she enthusiastically announced, 'And of course, I'll make your wedding dress, Kirsty, and don't worry, it'll be the most beautiful dress you'll ever see.'

Kirsty had to laugh at the older woman's excitement.

'Anybody would think it was you that was getting married, Mum.'

'It's just that I'm so happy for you, dear. Greg's a wonderful man. Kind, handsome, brave – what more could any girl want? You're very, very lucky. I hope you realise that, Kirsty.'

She realised it all right. But the next time she saw Greg it was in the fire station, and over a cup of coffee he proved yet again what an impatient man he was.

'Why don't we get married right away? Why wait until the summer? Summer seems a hell of a long time away.'

'Well, for one thing, Mum's making me a beautiful wedding dress and she's sewing it mostly by hand. It'll take her months. And it takes two years or more to book a wedding in any good hotel.'

'Why do you need a fancy dress? Why do we need a big wedding? I'd far rather drive to the local registrar's office now, just the two of us. No fuss, no crowds.'

'There isn't going to be a crowd. Unless you invite a crowd of firefighters. As far as I know, there's only going to be my mother, my father and my brother, Sandra and Tommy from the Art School, my Aunt Jess and a couple of your friends from the station.'

'By the way, did you speak to your brother about the gun?'

'Yes, don't worry. It's sorted.'

'It's you who does the worrying. You're constantly afraid he'll get himself into trouble. You're also continually worried in case he upsets your mother and gives her another heart attack.'

'Nonsense. Johnny adores Mum. And I'm fine, honestly. Everything's perfectly all right.'

She looked away and busied herself pouring coffee in order to avoid his eyes, in case he realised that she was lying.

Some of the other firefighters came noisily in then, and Kirsty retreated to the kitchen area to fetch more cups and another pot of coffee.

Coffee cups suddenly clattered across the table as there was a 'turn out', and once more the men raced into action. This time, it was a road traffic accident. A Honda Civic with a young man and woman inside had flipped when the driver tried to overtake on a corner. The car had rolled but was upright again. Broken glass was strewn across the road, sparkling in the sun. The roof of the Civic had collapsed in a crumpled concertina of metal. An ominous stain of blood smeared the driver's door. It was immediately obvious that the firefighters would need cutting gear. They'd had to be extra careful because there had been airbags – curtain airbags and headrest airbags – and if they cut through them, they could hit a cylinder and it could blow up.

Kirsty usually gathered what had happened from the talk between the firefighters as they swallowed a cup of coffee or some lunch on their return.

Greg talked about her constantly worrying about Johnny, but in fact she was becoming just as worried, if not more so, about him. Greg had been awarded several medals for bravery, but she guessed that at the root of his bravery could be the recklessness and impatience in his character. He would dash into any danger without a thought for himself. He was far too impatient to stand back and take his time considering and weighing up every aspect of any situation.

He had not just saved the lives of civilians in fires and accidents, but he had saved the lives of colleagues as well. They had a thing called a bodyguard, which, if a firefighter got injured and was not moving, went off automatically – and very loudly. This meant that the other firefighters stopped what they were doing and went straight to help their colleague.

Greg was often the first to reach the heart of the fire and drag the unconscious firefighter back to safety. They were all incredibly brave men who faced all sorts of dangers every day but who continued to devote their lives to helping people and keeping them safe.

Kirsty admired each and every one of them, but Greg was the most precious to her. She fervently prayed every night that he would be kept safe.

# IO

Sandra shook her auburn head at Tommy.

'I don't want any rent from you. We just need to share the living expenses, that's all. I was left this flat by my parents and so I haven't any rent to worry about. It's just bills like telephone and heating, that sort of thing. We can each pay our share and you've enough for that. You must have, because Greg charges you for rent and everything, doesn't he?'

'Yes, it's just I don't want to take advantage . . .'

'Don't be daft. We love each other. You want to be with me, don't you?'

'Yes, of course . . .'

'That's it settled then. I'll help you move your stuff.'

Tommy's thin face lit up with a smile.

'It'll be great, Sandra. I'm beginning to feel in the way at Greg's place. Oh, not that he purposely does anything . . .' he hastily added. 'It's just he's got Kirsty now and she's there so often, it's natural they want some privacy.'

It turned out that Tommy had very few belongings. The most he had was an easel and canvases and paints. As well as drawing and painting in the Art School, he worked a lot at home. There were sketches and paintings that Sandra admired so much that Tommy began to laugh at her.

'You're no judge of my stuff at all. You're completely biased in my favour.'

'No, I'm not. If I thought they were no good, I'd say so. Or at least I wouldn't sing their praises. I'm telling you, Tommy, you are a wonderful artist. You've got something, some sort of spark that even Simon Price doesn't have. Maybe that's one of the reasons he's so rotten to you. He's jealous.'

'Oh now, that's going too far. Everyone can see he's brilliant. If I practise until I'm a hundred, I'll never be as good as him.'

'You mustn't think like that, Tommy. Have some faith in yourself, for goodness' sake. Yours is a different style from his. You're more original.'

'Will you stop talking about my work. Come here.'

He gathered her into his arms, stroked her fiery hair and kissed it. His lips warmed over her neck and cheek. Then his mouth fastened over hers. She melted with love for him. But it was a protective love, as well as a passionate one. She resolved to do everything in her power to increase Tommy's confidence in his work, and not to allow Simon Price to continue to verbally destroy it. The more she thought about jealousy as a motivation, the more she believed it. He was using Tommy's unfortunate surname to get at him, but it was really that spark of originality and brilliance in Tommy's work that he couldn't stand.

It was good that Tommy liked her flat in Charing Cross Mansions. He was sorry, of course, that the M8 motorway had sliced apart the original soft, refined elegance of the area and Burnet's Charing Cross Mansions. The building, with its fine red sandstone and ornate frontage, was illuminated at night, making it a beacon of beauty. Sandra was proud to live in one of the flats, and now so was Tommy.

They'd had Greg and Kirsty to supper a couple of times, and it was good to share each other's happiness. It added to the enjoyment of the evening and they were all looking forward to the wedding. Greg was champing at the bit and would have rushed Kirsty to the registry office right away.

'Or,' he'd said, 'how about Gretna Green? How about us all going to Gretna? A double wedding. How about that?'

He was such an impatient, rash kind of man and obviously someone who liked getting his own way. But Kirsty wasn't going to be rushed. She was having none of it. Kirsty was no dumb blonde. She knew what she wanted and that was a white wedding next summer, to be held in the church.

As far as Sandra and Tommy were concerned, they had agreed that they were fine as they were, and would just wait until they'd finished Art School and had started earning a bit of money.

Kirsty's mother was making her wedding dress and Sandra wondered if she'd make her bridesmaid's dress as well. She couldn't afford an expensive, fancy dress. She was lucky, of course, to have the flat and no rent to worry about. She hadn't liked to ask Tommy but she didn't think his parents were helping him financially because he'd taken a part-time job at weekends in the local supermarket.

His parents were English but had retired and bought a house up in the north of Scotland, in Wester Ross. As far as Sandra knew, they had never been down to Glasgow to visit Tommy. She didn't think much of them at all. For a start, why didn't they change their name? Who in their right mind would want to go through life with a name like Pratt? She certainly didn't. Before she'd even think of marriage to Tommy, she'd have to persuade him to change his name. Of course, maybe it didn't have the same connotations in England. Maybe even in Scotland nobody bothered about it. Certainly none of the other students had said anything. It was just that evil bastard, Simon Price.

Anyway, Tommy seemed much happier once he'd moved

into Charing Cross Mansions. Apart from the view of the motorway and the ugly modern building on the other side of Sauchiehall Street and the equally awful coffin-shaped Union building, the flat had a good situation.

Sandra and Tommy liked to walk down Sauchiehall Street to their favourite café in the CCA, the Centre for Contemporary Art, where they could sit for ages over a cup of herbal tea and admire all the artwork. Sometimes they met some of the other students there. Everyone among their group was friendly and sociable, except Betty Powell.

'She's a loner, a right odd-bod.'

Quite often she could be found on her own, standing in the 'hen run', staring out over the city at the carpet of rooftops that undulated in waves away from the Art School, down towards the hidden Clyde. The occasional steeple stabbed the grey skies that loomed overhead. The hen run was one of the brilliant ideas of Charles Rennie Mackintosh. A dark stone staircase twisted and turned, punctuated by little archways like an Escher drawing all the way to the hen run. The hen run clung precariously to the edge of the massive stone building, a transparent floating capsule with its slanting glass roof and huge wall of glass.

Betty would just be standing there on her own. She never even turned to smile and say hello when a crowd of them passed, their feet clattering noisily along the old and increasingly rickety planking of the floor. She was an unattractive, bespectacled girl with her old-fashioned clothes, her pale unmade-up face and mousy frizz of hair. At first, they'd all tried to be friendly with her but she'd shrunk away, avoiding their eyes and saying very little, if anything. Eventually everyone gave up and just let her be.

Tommy had only been living in the flat for a few weeks when Sandra had the idea of being his life model. They had rigged up one of the spare rooms as a studio and they both

worked there. They couldn't afford a television but painting passed their time happily enough.

Tommy liked the idea and so each night, Sandra stripped off and leaned against the cushions of the small settee in the room, carefully draping her limbs into a pose of elegant casualness. She enjoyed the freedom and sensuality. Tommy, confident now that he was in his element, directed and painted her nakedness.

She could see, as he worked, the love in his eyes fading away, and total professional concentration taking its place.

But the love in her eyes never wavered.

# II

When Kirsty returned to the living room after getting a very drunken Johnny into bed, Greg was standing in the middle of the hearthrug, feet planted firmly apart, hands gripped behind his back.

'One day, Kirsty, you'll be forced to face facts.'

'What facts?' Her voice sharpened with protective anger. Johnny had come in with three of his Goth pals, all of them very drunk. Greg wasted no time in getting rid of the three pals. 'He's just been out enjoying himself with some of his friends. This was Paul and Renee's night off from the casino.'

'God knows what would have happened with those weirdos if I hadn't been here. As for your brother, Kirsty, he's a menace and a danger to himself, as well as everybody else.'

'You don't understand.'

How could Greg, always so confident, always so sure of himself, understand someone like Johnny?

'What's there to understand? As well as having weirdo friends, he's in charge of a car and a gun, for God's sake.'

'Don't be ridiculous, Greg. The gun's kept in the flat and he wouldn't have been capable of driving or doing anything in that state.'

'I'm being ridiculous?' Greg's voice rose with sarcasm.

'Kirsty, the guy's capable of anything and he knows you'll let him get away with anything.'

It was just that Greg didn't know him, she kept telling herself. He hadn't known Johnny as a sickly child unable to join in the games with other boys of his age. She remembered his hand in hers and his eyes saucer-sized with anxiety staring up at her as he said, 'When I'm a big boy, I'll be able to run faster than them, won't I, Kirsty? When I'm grown up, I'll be able to do anything better than them.'

He always tried so hard. Even as a child herself, she had seen the terrible fear in his eyes and she had hastened to reassure him.

'Of course you will,' she said, and kissed his painfully thin face.

The years had barely changed him. He still needed her reassurance, her protection, and her love, and nobody – not even Greg – could stop her giving her brother these things.

'You just don't know Johnny as I do, Greg.'

'I know he's a no-good weakling.'

No beating about the bush with Greg. Sometimes Kirsty had to laugh at his startling forthrightness. But she couldn't laugh now.

'How dare you say that!' she cried. 'He's got more kindness and compassion in his little finger than you'll ever have in your whole life, and he's none of your business.'

She knew she had gone too far as soon as the words flew out of her mouth. In her ensuing panic, she realised how much she loved Greg.

'Oh, I'm sorry Greg. I didn't mean that. I'm just upset.'

After a moment, Greg said, 'Let's get this straight.' His eyes were hard, and chillingly cold. 'When we get married, I don't want your brother causing any more trouble between us. That's why what he does, and what he is, is my business.'

She managed to nod and push out more apologetic words.

'I know, Greg. It's just that I was so worried about Mum waking up and hearing what was going on. Or Dad coming in. He's at some late meeting with the directors. And he'll have been drinking too. I just wanted Johnny to be in bed before Dad came home.' Fear filled her eyes. 'Please forgive me, Greg.'

'Of course I forgive you.' He pulled her into his arms. 'I love you and can't bear to see you worried and upset like this. The quicker we get married and you get out of this house and away from your brother, the better.'

'The time'll soon pass to our wedding date.' She hastily wiped at her eyes and smiled up at him. 'Sandra and Tommy are really looking forward to it and we're so lucky to get a hotel booking for the reception with a proper cake supplied and everything. As I told you, sometimes it takes a couple of years to get a wedding booking in such a good hotel.'

Greg sighed and shook his head.

'Well, I'm glad the lot of you are happy. You know how I feel. I would be more than happy to go to the nearest registry office. No cake, or any of the frills. Just a drink and then home afterwards.'

She gave him a friendly punch. 'That's just because you can't wait to get me into bed.'

He grinned. 'I get you into bed now. Or had you forgotten?'

As if she could. Since Tommy had left Greg's flat, and she and Greg could have the place to themselves, she had discovered just what a sexually passionate man Greg was.

Not for the first time, she told herself, she was an extremely lucky woman. She resolved never to mention Johnny's name to Greg again. It just led to arguments and trouble every time. The time might come when she would lose him. She daren't take that risk any longer. No, from now on, she told herself firmly, she was going to guard her relationship with Greg. From now on, she was definitely going to put him first.

That didn't mean, of course, that she was able to stop worrying about her brother. A few days later, she sensed a difference in him. So much so that she got him on his own in his bedroom, and said, 'Has something happened, Johnny? If there's something wrong, I don't want you to worry Mum about it. Just tell me.'

He gave a high-pitched laugh that made her more concerned than ever.

'Nothing's wrong.'

'You haven't got mixed up with anything dishonest, have you?'

'I haven't done a thing.' He laughed again. 'What an idea! What would your straight-as-a-die hero say to that? I can just imagine him rushing to tell his police pals all about me.'

Despite the laughter, she saw a glimpse of fear in his eyes before he turned away and left the room. She stood listening to his feet clattering down the stairs, wondering what she should do. He would be on his way now to Paul and Renee's flat. She thought about following him and confronting him there. She decided against it. He would be furious at her for putting a foot in their precious flat. To Johnny, it was almost a hallowed place. He always insisted it was the first job he'd managed to do successfully and where he was trusted and appreciated, where he was happy.

It would be wiser, Kirsty decided, to wait until tomorrow morning when he was at home and they could sit down and relax with a cup of coffee and have a proper talk. Her mother was always busy at her needlework and sewing machine in the forenoons. She hadn't seen her mother so happy and relaxed for years. Even her father couldn't spoil all the euphoria of the wedding plans.

What added to her mother's happiness, of course, was the fact that Greg was so good to the older woman. Kirsty had teased him about it.

'Who would believe,' she said, 'that a great big hulking brute could be so kind and gentle to an old woman?'

'Watch your language, my girl!' He glowered down at her with mock ferociousness. 'Or I'll be forced to put you over my knee and deliver some well-deserved corporal punishment. With this . . .' He showed her a big, broad palm. She laughed and smoothed her cheek against it.

'I'm not afraid of you.'

'Mmm.' He kissed her on the mouth. 'I must admit that for such a little, delicate-looking blonde, you've an astonishing amount of nerve.'

She had a feeling that she was going to need some of that nerve. Her instinct had always been right about Johnny. And her instinct was telling her now that something was seriously wrong. Johnny was not just anxious. He was frightened.

# 12

Betty pushed through the blackened swing doors into the studio. It was bathed in cool, clear light from the huge window that dominated the far wall, soaring up to the ceiling so high above them. She passed one of the other students. He was carrying his large canvas up the narrow wooden staircase to the spacious mezzanine work area that overlooked the main studio.

In the far corner, students were washing brushes in the old-fashioned deep sink. The wall behind it was smothered in a patina of generations of paint spattered and smeared in a riot of colour. Betty breathed in air redolent with the aroma of turpentine and linseed oil. She felt that this was where she belonged.

Then her happiness was suddenly punctured when the model appeared. She had expected Greg but it was a different firefighter. Admittedly, she knew that other firefighters took Greg's place from time to time. Word had got around the fire station that it was a good way of making extra cash. So, depending on their shifts, quite a few of them came in to take a turn at modelling for the Life class.

Betty Powell wasn't interested in any of the others. They lacked the charisma that Greg McFarlane possessed. The other firefighters were friendly and jolly, at the same time appearing awkward and embarrassed. None of them had Greg McFarlane's self-confidence and strength of will. She could see it in his hard stare, and the way he relaxed his body. There was no embarrassment in him. It was almost as if he flaunted his body, challenging others to feel sexually aroused by it. She certainly believed in that assessment of him and there was no doubt that he had succeeded in arousing her.

It continually amazed her that none of the other female students seemed to feel as she did, or experience any sexual arousal whatsoever. They treated all the firefighter models in exactly the same way. They concentrated on their canvases. Then during the breaks, they chatted to whatever model happened to be there about the local clubs or discos or their favourite music group.

It was as if she died each time Greg McFarlane wasn't there. When he was there, she couldn't keep her eyes off him, even during the tea breaks and lunch breaks. Then she felt she had to see him when he wasn't in the Art School. She didn't know where he lived, but one day she managed to follow him. She hailed a taxi and told the driver, 'Follow that blue Mazda.' Her heart pounded with the outrageousness of what she was doing. What if he saw her? When his car turned into Kirklee Terrace, she told the taxi driver to stop – just in time. Kirklee Terrace was a short, quiet street, and a taxi would have been more than obvious. Quickly she paid the driver and peered around to try to discern which house Greg McFarlane was about to go into.

She watched him park his car, then disappear into the very end door, the one next to the side entrance of the Botanic Gardens. What a wonderful place to live! How happy she could be with him there. After that day, every spare moment was spent following him. Sometimes she walked through the Gardens and loitered near the side entrance, watching the end doorway of the Terrace. Different people went in and out, but never Greg McFarlane. She would have to watch the fire station and somehow find out what shifts he was on, find out exactly where he went when he was neither working in the fire station nor at the Art School. But it was more difficult, she discovered, to watch the fire station and remain unseen. She had been nearby one day when she was startled by the fire engines suddenly clanging out and racing along the street. She caught a glimpse of firefighters sitting inside the vehicle dressed in their creamy gold-coloured firefighting uniforms. The vehicles passed out of her line of vision so quickly that she wasn't able to discern if Greg McFarlane was on one of the machines. She supposed he must have been because she had discovered that this was the station he worked at. She imagined the fire he must be speeding towards, the men, the women, the children he would be risking his life to rescue and carry to safety. She could hardly contain her admiration, her adoration of him.

She couldn't bear not seeing him, not being near to him. It was torture to waste precious time sitting in her mother's quiet house, listening to the monotonous tick-tock of the clock, and watching her mother neatly, endlessly sewing.

She made excuses as often as she dared. That the Art School had asked her to work late was the usual excuse, but her mother was beginning to query that. Something had to be done. Then she had the idea of making a hoax call and bringing the fire brigade out. She'd say there was a fire nearby, somewhere that she could watch the firefighters' arrival. Maybe even watch them from her mother's front window. She did make the call, very carefully of course, putting a handkerchief over the receiver to disguise her voice. She'd heard the riotous sound of the fire engines arriving and from behind the curtain, she peered out expectantly.

'What on earth are you doing, Betty?' her mother asked, coming into the room carrying the cake stand.

'I heard the fire engines. I just wondered where the fire was.'

'Well, it's not here, so sit down and take your tea before it gets cold.'

Betty could have wept with disappointment and frustration. Nothing, not even a fire, would be allowed to interrupt her mother's boring routines of a lifetime.

Then Greg appeared as a model again and at least she was able to devour him with her eyes during the School's art sessions. She could allow her imagination free rein and her creative art of poetry added to her intense pleasure and gratification.

His hands are tan and square.
I am close enough to see the dark, fine hairs
brushing the sides, and the pipe of a vein
embossing the skin in a braille of health.

His fingers are long, and curved
in relaxation. The index finger wears
a scraped knuckle with indifference
as if made raw in some menial task.

I can imagine his hands at work
aiming jets of water at a tower of hungry flame,
cradling the back of a child's head
while he carries her to safety.

His hands. My skin.
Stroking the skin on my arm,
providing a harmony of heat.
Not a moment too soon his hand moves
to other parts of me, not stopping
until the final, sharp, hot gasp.

Others in the art class
could be drawing a basket
of fruit for all the interest
worn on their faces.
I. I am elsewhere.

# 13

'That Betty Powell's awful odd, isn't she?'

They were in the bathroom together. Sandra had just come out of the shower and Tommy was spiking up his blond hair with gel.

'That's putting it mildly. Surely you don't need to ask that?'

'I know, but I mean, she's a real nutter. I caught her earlier in the Art School loo, before I left to come home. She had a lighted torch of paper. She hastily doused it under the tap and threw it into the bin as soon as she saw me. I said to her, "What do you think you're doing – trying to set the place on fire?" She scuttled away then without saying anything but she looked as guilty as hell.'

'My God!' Tommy cried out. 'That's really terrible. The place is Charles Rennie Mackintosh's greatest masterpiece.'

'Not to mention the people still in it who could have been killed before the fire brigade arrived.'

They both stared at each other for a long moment in silence. Then Sandra said, 'Have you seen the way she looks at Greg?'

'During break times, yes. I couldn't help noticing. It struck me as being creepy, to say the least.'

'I saw her the other day hanging around the side entrance of the Botanic Gardens.'

'You think she's stalking him?'

'I wouldn't be a bit surprised. But if she's thinking of trying to set fire to the Art School just to bring firefighters out, that's really dangerous. What do you think I should do? Report her?'

Tommy hesitated. 'The problem is that you've no proof, and she'll just deny everything. How about if we both speak to her? Give her a strong warning. Say that we know what she's up to and if she even thinks of trying such a thing again, or anything like it, we'll both report her and she'll be thrown out of the Art School and never get to come near the place again. She won't want to risk that.'

'No, she definitely won't want to lose her place in the Life class, gawping at Greg.'

'OK, we'll try that,' Tommy said. 'We'll certainly have to do something. I mean, that's why even smoking a cigarette is banned. That Art School is . . .'

'I know, I know. Charles Rennie Mackintosh'll be birling in his grave. But don't worry, we'll put the fear of death in her – never to dare try anything like that again.'

'It would have been bad enough if it had been a cigarette but you said it was a torch of paper?'

'Yes, it was like a rolled-up newspaper. It must have taken quite a deliberate effort to get it all burning. It was just as well that that tap spurts out such a strong gush of water. For a minute or two, I was really frightened.'

They had been invited to supper at Kirklee Terrace and on the way there, they decided to tell Greg and Kirsty about the incident.

Greg said, 'She didn't bother me. But this fire thing – that's different. That's not on.'

'We're going to make sure it doesn't happen again. Don't worry.'

Greg looked thoughtful. 'Where does she live?'

'Great Western Road.'

'We had a hoax call to a shop along near Anniesland yesterday.'

'That's where she lives.' Sandra's eyes widened. 'I once saw her walking towards the Cross. I was on my way to visit my auntie. My auntie used to live at Anniesland Cross.'

Greg said, 'I could tell my friends in the local police station. I'm especially friendly with Sergeant Jack Campbell there, as you know. But he'd need proof it was her. An awful lot of folk live around that area. It could have been anybody. And unfortunately we get quite a few hoax calls.'

'I bet it was her though.'

'Probably was. What the hell does she think she's doing?'

Tommy shrugged. 'Trying to get your attention probably. And to keep seeing you, even when you're not in the Art School.'

'She'll see me again all right, when I tell her to fuck off.'

'It's difficult though, isn't it? I mean, she's supposed to sit staring at you in the art class.'

'She's had that for a few days. I'm on duty.'

'Don't worry,' Sandra said. 'Tommy and I'll speak to her at the break.'

Kirsty laughed. 'What a carry on!'

Tommy obviously didn't see anything in the slightest bit amusing. 'That building, the Glasgow School of Art, is Charles Rennie Mackintosh's masterpiece. Even more so than his House on the Hill, or the House for an Art Lover. People come from all over the world to see the Art School. Staring at Greg won't do any harm, but trying to set fire to Charles Rennie Mackintosh's . . .'

'OK, OK.' Sandra gave him a playful punch. 'We've got the message. And I'm sure now that she's been found out, she won't try anything like that again.' She turned to the others. 'Tommy's mad about the place. Nobody dares say a word against it.'

'It's just that I appreciate art in any form. And of course Mackintosh was an artist as well as an architect. I feel very lucky to be able to study there and to have such a brilliant artist as a teacher.'

Kirsty groaned. 'You're even luckier not having him as a father.'

'You can't deny – nobody can deny, Kirsty – that your father is a brilliant artist.'

Greg shook his head. 'That's very noble of you, Tommy. After the way he treats you. If he spoke to me the way he speaks to you, I'd have punched his face in by now. Or broken his fingers one by one so that he could never hold a brush again.'

Tommy winced. 'Greg, for pity's sake, don't even think of such a thing. He just tells me the truth. I haven't a clue as a painter. I'm hopeless. He knows it and I know it.'

'Will you stop talking like that!' Sandra punched his arm again before turning to Kirsty. 'I know he's your father, Kirsty, but honest to God, it's really wicked the way he's been continuously undermining Tommy's self-confidence. I feel the same way as Greg. Forgive me, but I once reported him for the way he bullies everybody, but Tommy in particular. I got short shrift, of course. The powers that be just said we were lucky to have him as a tutor.'

'There you are. I told you we're lucky and me especially. I'm surprised they let me in the School in the first place.'

'Sandra's right, Tommy. He bullies us at home as well. He's nearly destroyed my brother, but he doesn't get away with it with me. I refuse to allow him to destroy my self-confidence, and you shouldn't allow him to destroy yours. He's charming to Greg, of course. He knows he couldn't get away with anything with him.'

Tommy didn't look convinced. Sandra loved him and longed to be able to comfort and help him. She kept desperately trying to think of something.

# 14

They pushed in through the double doors nearest Sauchiehall Street. The long oval wooden bar dominated the room. The gantry was covered with various bottles and speciality whiskies, and along the wooden fascia above the bar were inscribed various couthy sayings. Along the window wall were snug booths, facing into the main bar, where the tutors liked to sit for the early part of the evening when any business could be discussed. They always chose Tuesday because at nine-thirty a local blues band had a jam session in the far corner. This was always popular, not just for the quality of the group, which was indeed superb, but because of the fact that after forty minutes or so, pub regulars could join in, bringing out their own guitars, saxophones, or mouth organs.

The standard of the amateurs was always surprisingly good and, because you could never predict who would turn up with what instrument, it gave the evening a real vibrancy. All tied together beautifully with the rasping vocals of the lead singer, a small, slender, middle-aged man with a voice straight from a ghetto in the deep south.

The pub was crowded. Crushed round a table cluttered with pint glasses, some of the directors and tutors were already enjoying a drink and a talk. The main topic of conversation was the different groups of students and how they were progressing.

'One thing that gets nowhere with me,' Simon Price said, 'is the sycophantic idiots who think they'll get a good crit if they buy me a few drinks.'

One of the others laughed. 'I know. I get them as well. Doesn't stop me enjoying the drinks, though. A good pint's a good pint, no matter who pays for it.'

Simon Price remained serious. 'I'm only interested in genuine talent. In one lot I go to, there's this guy, Tommy Pratt. Now he has real talent but he's needing toughened up. As you can imagine, he's going to get a lot of stick with a name like that, for a start. And, like all of us had at the beginning, he's going to get rejections and God knows what else to put him down.'

One of the others rolled his eyes and groaned. 'Don't remind me. One guy said about me that I'd never get anywhere and he could paint better than me. He was a bloody journalist, for God's sake.'

A director said, 'You think this Pratt boy has got something special then, Simon?'

'Yes, definitely. But he's such a soft mark. He's got no guts. No stand up and fight. He's likely to pack everything in at the first bad review.'

'Well,' the director laughed, 'if anyone's able to toughen him up and make him hang on in there, it'll be you.'

'Writers are the same,' somebody else said. 'J. K. Rowling's *Harry Potter* was turned down by nineteen publishers before she got accepted. That's guts for you.'

'Yeah,' Simon agreed. 'Pratt would have given up after the first rejection. But I'm determined to make a man of him, if only because I don't want the brilliant paintings he could do never to materialise.'

'It must have been from the group he's in that a girl came to me and complained that you were picking on him.'

'Oh aye, that would be Sandra Matheson, a red-haired girl. She's got him shacking up with her in her flat in Charing Cross

Mansions. It would be better if she concentrated on her own work instead of distracting Tommy from his.' Price got up. 'It's my round, I think. The same again for everybody?'

He went over to the bar counter and had a tray filled with pints of beer and a glass of soda and lime for Joe Brownlie, who had a stomach ulcer and, for the time being at least, was forbidden any alcohol.

Returning to the table, Price passed the glasses around. 'I don't know how you can drink that stuff, Joe.'

'It's what the bloody job has done to me and could do to you as well. The doctor said it was stress-related.'

'Oh well, we're all in danger of that. So we'd better enjoy our beer while we can.' He raised his glass. 'Cheers.'

'It doesn't help not being able to have a smoke,' Joe said. 'I'm in bloody agony here.'

'Did the doctor not ban that as well?'

'Oh aye, but I had to draw the line at that. I've been a smoker since I was a teenager and it's impossible to give up. I tried but I'm telling you, the withdrawal symptoms are worse than when you give up drugs.'

One of the other tutors said, 'There's more than a few of the students on drugs. Some on cannabis, some on ecstasy, I think, and I suspect a few idiots have reached the heroin stage. But what can you do? Except to hope they grow out of it.'

'Well, we did, right enough. Most of us dabbled in something when we were young, didn't we? I know I did a bit of experimenting.'

'It's different now. There's more stuff around and much stronger stuff. It's too often not a case of just dabbling or experimenting. Some of them are in danger of getting seriously addicted.'

'That's true, and they could ruin their lives and their talent. But as you say, what can we do? If we start preaching about that, they won't listen. It might even make them worse.'

Price took a big swig of his beer, then wiped his moustache with the back of his hand. 'Well, I've one consolation with the Pratt boy. As far as I can tell, he's not on drugs. He's too serious about his work for any of that. I don't think he'd risk anything that would spoil his concentration.'

One of the others laughed. 'What about that red-haired girl? She's the one who's liable to be a stronger distraction than drugs. She might even persuade the lad to start on them.'

'Over my dead body,' Simon Price growled.

# 15

Kirsty could never resist looking at the glass case outside the entrance of the fire station. It contained the embalmed body of a dog called Bruce. He had lived at the fire station from 1894 until his death. His first appearance was thought to have been at some sort of procession, where he had attached himself to one of the city's fire engines and followed it back to the station. Soon his owner found out where he was and took him home. But a few hours later, Bruce had returned to the fire station and stayed there as a full-time, unpaid member of the Brigade. His licence was actually paid for by Glasgow Corporation for the rest of his life. He would always lie quietly in the watch room, then the moment the alarm bell rang, he would be up and away to the fire, running some twenty or thirty yards in front of the horses that were drawing the appliances. Most people were puzzled at how he always seemed to know the way to an outbreak and thought he must have an amazing instinct. What actually happened was that the driver of the leading appliance would indicate the direction to follow by nodding or signalling with his whip and the dog, glancing back, was quick to see which way to turn.

Apparently when one old lady was visiting the station, she noticed that Bruce had a sore paw. As a result, she ordered a set of four small rubber boots to be delivered to the station. But Bruce had not been very keen on them and preferred his naked paws. He continued to run to fires until his death in 1902 and now there he was, still in the fire station, and with his rubber boots by his side.

Sometimes Kirsty came in by another door but she preferred this entrance because her heart was always touched by seeing Bruce and being reminded of his story. It was obvious that, despite the firemen being just as tough as today's firefighters, they had been fond of Bruce and good to him, and couldn't bear to part with him, even in death. That's why they had him embalmed so that they could continue to keep him near to them in the station.

When she reached the watch room, and the adjoining kitchen area, there were men in the gym area. Some were heaving at the weights machines. There were machines to develop and harden the upper-arm muscles and shoulders, others for the back of the legs, others for the chest. An hour was allocated at the end of each shift for exercise. Of course, if the alarm bell went, they rushed off to whatever emergency it was. But they needed to try and get whatever part of the hour they could before going off duty. It was vitally important to be strong because so much of the gear they had to lift and carry about and use was excessively heavy.

Kirsty had seen Greg the night before and she was looking forward to seeing him again when he came in for the day shift. The exercise machines had certainly worked for him. Every muscle in his body was bulky and hard and perfectly shaped. No wonder all the students in the Art School enjoyed drawing and painting him.

Sandra had told her, 'Even your father, Kirsty, said Greg had a perfectly formed body. Have you seen Tommy's painting of him?'

She hadn't. She kept well clear of the Glasgow School of

Art. She had enough of her father at home without seeing him at the Art School.

But she'd seen examples of Tommy's other work when she and Greg had visited Sandra and Tommy at the flat at Charing Cross Mansions. It was obvious that Sandra and Tommy were in love but Kirsty always detected the sadness in Tommy's eyes. Sandra confided in her that Tommy was suffering from fits of depression. Sandra blamed Kirsty's father's continuous criticism and ridicule of Tommy and his work.

'I'm sorry to speak about your father like this, Kirsty, but I absolutely hate and despise the man for the way he treats Tommy.'

'You don't need to apologise to me,' Kirsty said. 'I know only too well what my father's like. I just wish there was something I could do to help Tommy. I'm no artist but even I can see Tommy has talent. There can't be any doubt about that. It seems to me he's got something extra. I don't know what it is but his work seems to glow from the canvas, seems to come to life as you look at it.'

'I know. I know. That's exactly it,' Sandra cried out. 'I keep telling him that but he thinks I'm biased because of how I feel about him.'

'I'll tell him as well.'

'Thanks Kirsty. It's worth a try but I bet he'll just think I put you up to it. I mean, he'll smile and thank you but he won't really believe you. Your father has got him too brainwashed into thinking differently. I'm getting really worried. He gets so depressed. He just kind of sinks into himself and goes quiet and I feel he's not close to me any more. Not close to anybody.'

'I could try and speak to my father if you want. But I'm sure that wouldn't do any good. It would just give him an excuse to have a go at me. I could put up with that. I'm used to him having a go at me, but the thing is that it wouldn't do

Tommy any good. The danger is in fact that he'd be even worse to him.'

'Oh God, no. We don't want to risk that.'

'Why does he do it, I wonder? I mean, keep putting people down?'

'Let's face it, Kirsty. He's a bully and it makes bullies feel big. They don't do it so much, if at all, to stronger characters. He's charming to all the directors, for instance, because they're in a stronger position than him, for a start.'

'You're right. He never tries anything with Greg. He knows he wouldn't get away with anything with him. He's even as charming as can be to me and Mum when Greg's around. He waits until Greg's safely away before being his nasty, sneery self again. You should hear how he is with my brother, Johnny. He doesn't get the chance so much now because Johnny works every evening, but for years he was unspeakably cruel to poor Johnny. I keep trying to make up for it by being as supportive as I can.' She worriedly bit her lip. 'But it's not easy, and Greg doesn't understand.'

'Greg'll just be putting you first.'

'I know.'

'He's obviously crazy about you, Kirsty.'

'I'm not complaining and I know I should put him first too. I do try but . . .' She hesitated unhappily. 'But Johnny's my brother. We've grown up together, and he's suffered so much. Not only from our father, but with terrible ill health.'

Once more she tried to convince herself that she must put Greg first as she prepared the breakfasts for the men. Soon they were lining up at the hatch and she was dishing up the cooked meals, hoping at the same time that they would have peace to eat it. So often, there was a turn out and they all had to immediately race off and fly down the poles and out to the yard, where their boots waited inside the legs of their protective trousers, so that they could just quickly step into the boots and hoist up the trousers.

The gaffer or crew manager would have collected the job details from a computer at one of the entrances. This told him exactly where the fire or road accident or other emergency was and all the other details they needed. They would grab on the rest of their uniform, including their helmets and the heavy breathing apparatus that the two firefighters sitting on the outside had to wear. They'd go in and fight the fire, and rescue people.

Every time there was a turn out, Kirsty had a tension headache with anxiety. She told him this, and how it was made worse by her belief that he was too impatient and reckless, and as a result could cause more danger to himself.

'No, no, darling, you've got it wrong. When I'm on duty, I respond in a professional manner because I've had the training. You must go in and do the job you're trained for and as I say, you do it in a professional manner. We all do.'

He had come on duty now and when she smiled lovingly at him, he winked at her before joining a noisy group of men at one of the tables.

# 16

Betty thankfully escaped from the gloom of her mother's house and made her way eagerly towards the Glasgow School of Art. Another day of intimacy with Greg McFarlane to look forward to. 'I'm sure he's beginning to notice me,' she thought, and her creative imagination ran ahead of her.

I feel it's like he noticed me
for the first time that day.
As his eyes settle on mine with recognition,
he offers me a small smile.

He sits, once again wearing Adam's suit,
leaning back against the cushion of the chair.
His legs stretched out in front of him, crossed
at the ankles, his penis resting on his thigh.

In my head, at least, Mother's voice is dead.
The grey stone of my mother's will rolling
across the floor of my mind,
coming to rest in the darkest corner.
I feel the string that binds me loosen.
My heart is thrumming. My mind
alive with the possibilities of him.

Out walking. Late. With streetlamps
our only company. My head
leaning into his shoulder.
My mind tasting the charge of sweetness.
Walking blindly. My leg bumping against his.
His, 'Sorry'. My laugh.
A sound he inhales when he kisses me.
Two figures under an electric light.
Bright with desire.

She pushed through the doors of the Art School. Happy. Happy.

She was the first arrival and wasted no time in setting up her easel. The others came trickling in one at a time, chatting and laughing. Except blond-haired Tommy Pratt and red-haired Sandra Matheson. They looked very serious.

Then, what a disappointment! The model who appeared was not Greg. It was one of the other firefighters. It took Betty all her effort not to burst into tears. She felt devastated, gutted. After her earlier euphoria, the day stretched before her, long and lonely. And all she had left to look forward to after the Art School was her tight-lipped mother waiting with her soul-destroying routine that never changed. She wanted to go to the fire station and watch for Greg. Or go to the Botanic Gardens and stand near the side entrance and watch for him coming back to his house. Her mother, however, was getting annoyed about her going out in the evening or coming home late for tea.

She had tried to tell her mother that she had to go looking for special threads or material for her embroidery class, or that the tutor had asked everyone to stay late for a special part of the embroidery lesson. It was beginning to make her mother resentful of the Art School and she was even beginning to threaten to go to the embroidery tutor and complain.

'It's time I was going to that Art School to have a word with your tutor.'

'No, no, Mother. It'll be all right, I promise.'

For her mother to go anywhere near the Art School would be disastrous, and had to be avoided at all costs.

And so she had just to go home straight from the Art School and her disappointment at Greg not being there. She had to sit and watch her mother set the small table with the rose-patterned china teacups, saucers, plates, sugar bowl and cream jug. A neatly folded linen napkin was carefully positioned on each plate. The silver cutlery was neatly placed. Then the three-tiered cake stand. Buttered scones on the top, Victoria sponge on the middle, and biscuits on the bottom. Next came the silver teapot, from which her mother carefully poured tea into the cups.

It was enough to drive anyone mad.

She was beginning to have longings and dreams about her mother dying. How wonderful it would be to have perfect freedom to do exactly as she liked, where and whenever she liked.

But it looked as if, despite being in her fifties and despite the unhealthy-looking blotches of colour on her face, her mother and all her endless routines would go on forever. Betty had never been lucky. Right from early childhood, as far back as she could remember, she had been repressed, manipulated, eroded by this selfish woman and her twisted view of life and men and sex.

As she sipped her tea and tried to ignore the monotonous tick-tock, tick-tock of the clock, her mind darted this way and that trying to think of some way to escape from the house for at least an hour or two so that she could see Greg. She couldn't think of anything that would at the same time prevent any danger of her mother going near the Art School. The horror of her mother finding out that she had never taken embroidery, but was instead in the life-drawing class in the same room as a naked man – actually sitting looking at him and painting him – was too much to cope with. Her hand trembled at the mere idea, making her teacup rattle in its saucer.

'Is something wrong?' her mother queried.

'No, no. Sorry.'

'You haven't had your scone yet.'

Picking up a scone, she thought bitterly, 'Oh yes, of course. That's what's wrong with me. I haven't had my scone yet.' Her stomach tightened at the thought of eating it, and then the Victoria sponge, and then the biscuits.

Once her mother was dead and gone, she'd never even look at these things again. She'd break all the china and smash the three-tiered cake stand, fling the silver into the bin and set the embroidered tea cloth on fire.

Thinking of fire brought Greg into her mind again. She wondered when his shift would change and he'd be back modelling. An awful thought struck her. She'd heard the firefighters just did modelling jobs when they were short of money. What if Greg wasn't short of money any more? What if he never came back to the Art School? If he didn't appear tomorrow, she would have to go over to the West End and try to find him. She would slip out of the class and the School early. Or pretend she was feeling ill and had to go home. Then she'd go to the fire station and wait for him. Maybe if he saw her, he'd realise how she felt. He'd understand and it would bring them closer.

Her euphoria began to return and with it, the words of the poem she'd created earlier.

> Two figures under an electric light.
> Bright with desire.

# 17

Sandra and Tommy left Charing Cross Mansions and strolled hand in hand along Sauchiehall Street. They were on their way to the Art School. Later they planned to spend some time in the Mitchell Library in North Street. Just to see the Mitchell illuminated in the evening was a thrill. Its glorious dome was splashed with golden light against the purple sky as it soared proudly over the teeming traffic of the motorway. Tommy appreciated it almost as much as the Charles Rennie Mackintosh buildings.

'It's not nearly as original, of course. But then Mackintosh was a genius. No one could compare with him. But the Mitchell is pretty imposing. It's the Renaissance palace of literature. Did you know it was founded by a tobacco lord, Stephen Mitchell?'

Sandra shook her head. 'But I know it's got the largest reference collection in Europe.'

'My favourite is the Burns collection. I love spending time in the Burns room. Now there was another genius.'

There was a café in the Mitchell where they planned to have a coffee and something to eat later. Soon they were passing the towering Baird Hall, an Art Deco building which they both admired.

'Glasgow's really great for architecture of all kinds.'

Sandra agreed but said, 'I know but you've always got to tell visitors they have to go around looking up.'

They had decided they would corner Betty Powell during the lunch break. That way they would be able to have more time and a better chance of privacy.

It was one of the other firefighter models who was sitting, and right away, Sandra noticed that for once, Betty was not the first student in the classroom eagerly setting up her easel. That obviously was because the model was not Greg McFarlane.

Greg had told them he would be on early watch for the next few days.

They all worked diligently until lunchtime, except for a short coffee break mid-morning. Simon Price, as usual, never missed a chance of having a dig or a sneer at Tommy. Since Tommy had come to live with Sandra and they were really close, she could see how deeply this treatment affected him. He tried to put up a cheerful front but the terrible sadness in his eyes never changed. Often when Sandra came into the room unexpectedly, she would get a glimpse of the hopeless droop of his shoulders and the disappointed twist of his mouth, before he straightened and smiled at her.

At lunchtime, they both went over to Betty, and Sandra said, 'Betty, we're both here to give you a serious warning.'

Immediately Betty tried to hurry away but Tommy caught her arm and stopped her.

'Look, both Sandra and I know you've been following Greg, stalking him in fact. Not only that, you've been making hoax calls to the fire brigade. Even worse, you've tried to set the Art School on fire.'

Betty's pale face had gone a sickly shade of grey and her eyes were panicking around, desperate to see any means of escape.

'It's got to stop, Betty,' Sandra said, 'or we're going to report you and that'll mean you'll be lucky if you don't get arrested. But you'll certainly be chucked out of the Art School for good. You'll never be allowed to set foot in the place again.'

Tommy cut in then. 'What's more, we've already told Greg and he's absolutely furious. He wanted to report you right away but Sandra and I have managed to persuade him to wait and give us a chance to talk to you first. Are you listening to us? Do you want to go to jail or be banned from the School?'

'It's definitely going to be one or the other or both if you ever go near Greg again. Surely you must know you haven't a chance with him. He hates your guts.'

'And don't dare even think of setting fire to any place,' Tommy said.

At that point, Betty managed to free herself and escape.

They didn't bother to follow her.

Tommy said, 'That should have done the trick. We couldn't have made it much stronger.'

'I know. We've scared the wits out of her.'

'I can't help feeling sorry for her in a way.'

'For goodness' sake, Tommy, don't go soft on me now. If you must feel sorry for someone, feel sorry for poor Hamish Ferguson getting beaten up. Not to mention his ghastly digs.'

'I know, but Betty's obviously not a happy girl.'

'Just forget about it now. We had to stop her, for everyone's sake. Just imagine what would have happened if she had managed to set the School on fire. Lots of people would have been killed.'

'Right enough. It doesn't bear thinking about.'

'Well, stop thinking about it. It's sorted.'

Nevertheless, they were both feeling a bit stressed for the rest of the afternoon. So much so that at one point when Simon Price was picking on Tommy, Sandra lost her temper and cried out, 'For God's sake, you're putting us all off with your constant sniping at Tommy.'

The tutor's moustache quivered with anger.

'I'll have none of your impertinence, girl. I know you've ghastly red hair, but that's no excuse.'

At the end of the session, Sandra said to Tommy, 'I don't feel like going to the Mitchell now, do you? Yet I don't feel like going straight home either.'

Tommy agreed.

'How about going to Greg's place and letting him know how we got on? He should be off duty and at home by the time we get over to the West End.'

'OK.'

They didn't feel like walking either and so they took the bus to the Botanic Gardens and began walking through the gardens towards the side entrance, and Greg's place in Kirklee Terrace. The Botanic Gardens was a beautiful place and it made them feel better. They passed the stunning Kibble Palace, a glass temple with its ribbed dome sweeping up over the exotic plants that nestled around its base.

'Maybe Greg arranged to go straight to Kirsty's.'

'Well, we'll soon see.' Tommy opened the side gate and they both went up the few steps fronting Greg's building.

Thankfully for them, he was at home and the door opened to allow them in. They wasted no time in telling him how they had, as Sandra said, 'Scared the wits out of Betty Powell. She won't be bothering you again, Greg.'

'She'd better not. She won't know what's hit her if I've to deal with her. For a start, I've no time for anyone who makes hoax calls. While the fire engines are out on one of them, somebody else might be in real need of our help. Somebody might burn to death while the engine's out on a hoax call.'

'As I say, you can be sure she won't do anything like that again!'

# 18

Betty ran and ran and ran. And ran. She didn't know where. Until, exhausted and choking for breath, she found herself outside the Royal Concert Hall. She leaned against its wall, struggling to calm her breathing. Eventually, she was able to cross Killermont Street and go into the Buchanan Bus Station. There were some seats in the middle of the concourse and she collapsed onto one. People were milling around buying tickets, studying timetables, buying sweets and newspapers and bottled water. In the open-fronted café, people were sitting drinking tea and eating sandwiches. In the middle of the concourse, next to where she sat, there was a sculpture of a young soldier with his girlfriend hanging around his neck. She was wearing the soldier's beret and her heels were kicking up joyously behind her. The world was going on exactly as usual. Except her world.

She could hardly believe what had happened. Everybody knew everything. Or so it seemed. And Greg hated her. And she was in danger of losing her place at the Art School. But that was her life. She couldn't exist without it. Yet at the same time she didn't know how she could go back. It would be an ordeal facing everyone again. Especially Greg. Oh, how she had been fooling herself, imagining that he could be attracted to her and longing to be with her as much as she longed to be with him. It had all been merely a figment of her over-developed imagination. And her desperate need.

She certainly didn't feel able to go back right now. Best to go home, give herself a bit of time to recover, and return tomorrow as if nothing had happened. She'd make some excuse to her mother about why she was home early. As far as she knew, the model tomorrow was to be one of the other firefighters, not Greg. That would give her time to douse her feelings, or at least get a grip of them and hide them deep, deep down inside so that he would never see them. From now on, she must hide her feelings from everyone. And outside of the School, she mustn't be seen near Greg. Tears were threatening to build up inside her now at the thought of Greg hating her and of not being able to be near him.

Somehow, she found her way to a bus that would take her home. She sat breathing deeply and continuing her fight to keep the tears at bay. She entered the draughty tiled close and climbed the stairs to her mother's flat. She fumbled for her key, and once the door was open and she was in the lobby with its dark brown varnished wallpaper, she called out as her mother always told her to do, 'It's Betty, Mother.'

It was part of the usual routine.

Then her mother would call back, 'Wash your hands. I'm just bringing in the cake stand.'

Right from childhood, she had always to wash her hands before sitting down to any meal.

'Wash your hands. Tea's almost ready.'

Only this time there was no answering call of any kind.

It was another shock in her terrible day. A small shock, but a shock nevertheless.

'Mother?'

She reached the sitting room. The fireside table was not set. It was not even covered by the embroidered tea cloth. She went into the kitchen. There was no one there. The bedroom, the bathroom, every corner of the flat was silent and empty. Then the jangle of the phone startled her. She nervously picked up the receiver. No one ever phoned them.

'Betty Powell?' a voice queried.

'Yes.'

'I think you'd better come to the Art School right away. Your mother's here and she doesn't look well.'

Horror upon horrors!

This was the worst of all. She felt so physically weak now, she had to get a taxi to take her to the Art School.

The embroidery tutor was waiting in the janitor's office in the downstairs hall.

'You're Betty Powell, aren't you?' The tutor immediately pounced on her.

'Yes.'

'Your mother was obviously confused and came into the embroidery class asking for you. I had to explain that you've never been in my class, but I was sure I'd seen you going into the Life class and you know how easy it is to get lost here if you're not used to the place. So I took her there.'

Betty could imagine her mother's shock being much worse than anything her daughter had suffered that day. Now Betty had no idea how she could face her mother. What on earth could she say? What excuse could she make for all the deceit? What excuse for wanting to paint naked people, but worse – oh, much worse – naked men?

Impossible. She was about to turn away and go back to the bus station, take a bus to London or anywhere else at all, and never see her mother or her mother's house again, when the tutor put her arm around her shoulders.

'I'm sorry, but she got worse and we had to send for an ambulance. I phoned you again but got no answer. So I knew you must be on your way here. I'll get a taxi now to take you to the hospital.'

Betty nodded and all that broke the silence until the taxi arrived was the sound of the outside doors opening and closing, and the scuffing of students' feet going in and out.

'I hope everything turns out all right, dear,' the tutor said. 'Let me know how you get on.'

Betty no longer knew what to think. Her brain and her emotions had taken such a battering, and all on the one day. It was too much.

She found her way through the hospital to where she was told her mother was. Outside the ward, the nurse explained, 'I'm sorry, Miss Powell. Your mother has suffered a stroke. Fortunately, she was brought in very promptly, and so she's as well as can be expected, but I'm afraid it has affected her speech. She's conscious but unable to speak.'

Betty began to tremble.

'Would you like a glass of water, dear?'

'Thank you.'

'Sit down for a minute or two and I'll fetch one for you.'

Betty sat trying to compose herself. The icy cold drink helped.

It could not be put off any longer and so she followed the nurse into the ward to the bed where her mother was propped up by pillows into a sitting position.

'Hello, Mother.' She sat down on the chair next to the bed. 'I'm sorry you're not well.' Her voice sounded unexpectedly calm, not like her voice at all. It certainly did not reflect how she felt inside.

She didn't kiss the older woman. They had never kissed. Even when she was a child. Perhaps because she was the product of a coupling with a man and therefore must have a bit of a man in her, that was why her mother had kept her distance and had been unable to show any affection. For the first time, she wondered what her mother's mother had been like. Had that grandmother she never knew been a person with the same unnatural disgust and hatred of men and sex as her mother?

Now her mother's eyes, dark and sunken, stared at her with unmistakable disgust and hatred. Their dark hollows made a startling contrast to the whiteness of her hair, no longer pinned back but straggling loose and long down either side of her face. She looked like an evil witch.

'I'm sorry,' Betty said, 'that you had to find out about my course at the Art School the way you did. I never meant you to be upset.' She fiddled with her spectacles and tried to avoid the dark accusing stare. 'But you see, I never liked embroidery and I got this chance of attending the Life class. I thought if you didn't find out and I got my degree, you'd just be happy with that. There was really no need for you to know.'

She wondered what was going to happen. Obviously she couldn't take her mother home like this. She supposed they would eventually tell her at the hospital if and when her mother would be able to return home.

Now she rose. There was no point in staying just to carry on a one-sided conversation.

'I'll come back to see you as soon as I can,' she said before leaving.

The flat was coldly silent when she returned. She went into the kitchen and put the kettle on for tea. Then she felt a sudden rush of emotion, a wave that swept through her and sent adrenalin pumping through her arteries. She lifted the cake stand, paused for a second, then sent it crashing to the tiled kitchen floor, breaking each of the plates into jagged pieces that seemed to mirror her emotions. Then, one by one, she dropped every piece of the china tea set.

# 19

'I feel terrible now, don't you?' Tommy said.

'What about?'

'What do you think? About Betty Powell, of course.'

'Why should you feel terrible about her?'

Tommy rolled his eyes.

'Don't kid on you don't know about her mother. Everyone's talking about it.'

'I know Betty Powell's one hell of a liar. Fancy having her mother think she's been in the embroidery class of all places, and for all this time.'

'It's why she felt she had to do that that bothers me.'

'Tommy, will you stop thinking about her? I've told you before, if you must feel sorry for somebody, feel sorry for somebody like Hamish Ferguson or Kirsty. Her life must be hell with a father like Simon Price.'

'He might be all right at home with his family. I mean, compared to how he is at the Art School. He gets on to me so much because of my failure to reach proper standards in my work.'

'Proper standards? You're a better painter than he is, that's the trouble.'

'Sandra, don't be ridiculous.'

'I'm not. OK, he's a good painter but you've got originality,

Tommy. There's a spark of something extra, something different, in your work.'

Tommy shook his head.

'There's something different, all right. I wish I knew what it was so that I could tackle it properly and get it right. I'm never going to get my degree at this rate.'

'You will. You will. Never mind what Price says. Have faith in yourself. By the way, Kirsty was raving about the portrait of me. She just loves it, and so do I.'

'Good.' He smiled. 'I'm glad about that.' He didn't sound in the least glad. His voice had gone flat and he had acquired the air of hopelessness that Sandra noticed had been increasing recently. She didn't know what to do with him. She kept desperately trying to boost his self-confidence but nothing seemed to work. Even when she lost her temper, it only made him more loving towards her. He told her how much he appreciated her faith in him, how much he loved everything about her. He'd grin and add, 'Even that wild temper and that fiery hair.'

Sometimes, when he was in one of his spells of silent hopelessness, Sandra wondered if she dared to suggest that he went to see a doctor. Maybe a doctor could give him some sort of antidepressant drug. He definitely needed help of some sort. Then, one night in bed, he actually burst into tears in her arms.

'Tommy, you're suffering from serious depression. You need medical help, darling. Please make an appointment with the doctor. Or I can make it for you. I'll go with you as well.'

Tommy rubbed away his tears with the sheet.

'I'm sorry. I'm making a right fool of myself. I don't know how you put up with me, Sandra. You've the patience of a saint.'

'Me?' Sandra howled with derision. 'The patience of a saint? Don't be daft. I'm the most impatient, quick-tempered person imaginable. It's just that I'm worried about you, Tommy. You're suffering from depression but there's nothing to be ashamed about in that.'

'Well, I am ashamed. It's true what Simon Price says. I'm a hopeless weakling.'

'Simon Price. Simon Price. What the hell does he know about anything?'

'He knows about art and who has talent and who hasn't.'

'Tommy, how many times must I tell you? He's a bully and he's picked on you because you let him get away with it. It's got nothing to do with what he knows about art.'

'You can't deny he's a brilliant artist, Sandra. Nobody can.'

'OK, he's a good artist. I never said he wasn't. But he bullies you, Tommy. Nobody can deny that. Ask any of the others. It's not just my opinion.'

Tommy turned away. 'I'm sorry for acting like a kid. Now let's just forget all this and get to sleep.'

Sandra teetered on the verge of losing her temper and flaying his naked back with wild punches. Only with superhuman effort did she roll on to her other side, close her eyes and say nothing.

It was impossible to get through to Tommy. She wondered if she should go to the doctor and just tell him about Tommy and ask him to give her the necessary medications. But she knew in her heart that she was fooling herself. The doctor would not hand out drugs to her. He'd tell her he'd have to see the patient. He'd insist that Tommy would have to come to the surgery and speak to him.

She wondered if she should have another go at persuading Tommy to see sense. But she'd been trying her best for what seemed like ages to do that. She just could not get through to him. In fact, she was beginning to fear that Tommy would get sick of her nagging at him and withdraw from her – completely withdraw. Stop loving her, even.

She couldn't bear for that to happen. Yet her desperation to help him wouldn't go away. She tossed and turned in bed, unable to sleep, as her worry and anxiety grew until she felt quite ill herself. Of course, everything always felt worse at night, she told herself. She would see everything differently in the morning and feel much happier.

But she didn't really believe it, and in her ensuing nightmare-filled sleep, terrible things loomed black on the horizon.

# 20

A phone call had gone in to control. The control operator (at Johnstone) took all the details and sent out a PDA, a pre-determined attendance, to Queen Margaret Drive station because a road traffic collision had been reported in their area.

The alarm bells filled the station with clamorous noise. Kirsty always jerked in fright when she heard them. Greg was flexing his muscles on one of the machines in the gym area. His back was braced against the padded support of the pec deck, his arms pulled back like some sort of crucifixion, as he slowly flexed his chest muscles, bringing his arms together. When he heard the alarm, he leapt from the machine and raced towards the room where all their protective clothing was laid out in readiness.

Downstairs, a printer called a fire card was already printing through the details of the address, the location, and on this occasion the information that it was a road collision, the vehicle was on fire, and there was a person trapped inside.

Someone took the slips off the machine and rushed with them to the appliance so that the guys had all the details.

Firefighters flew down the poles, landed on the rubber mat, then ran out to the fire engine. They frantically clawed their way into boots and their ochre-coloured jackets and trousers.

Helmets were slammed onto heads as they hauled themselves onto the engine. The huge engine burst forward and swung hard left out into the busy roadway, its siren screaming out a warning. Speed was of the essence. If life was in danger, they had to get to the location as quickly as possible. More often than not, they risked their own lives in their efforts to do so. Carved in the wall above one of the doors of the Queen Margaret Drive fire station was a long list of names of men who had died while fighting fires, attending road accidents and saving people's lives.

Traffic blurred by as they thundered along the road, the engine swaying alarmingly as it swung from side to side, narrowly avoiding the cars that pulled over to let it pass. They slammed hard down into a pothole with teeth-jarring force. Hands gripped the metal supports with knuckles showing white with the strain. The lights were red directly in front of them and, siren howling, they barely slowed as the engine rocketed through. Instinctively, Greg braced his legs in nervous expectation until they were through the lights. Up ahead, they could see a pall of black, oily smoke.

They slewed to a halt near the blazing car and, although it was heavily blackened at the front and partially concealed by the smoke, it was obviously a Mini, and of a sickly yellow colour. With a sense of dread, Greg looked at the number plate.

On approaching the fire, they could see the charred remains of a body inside. The victim was obviously dead and in that scenario, the firefighters had just to leave the body and concentrate only on putting out the fire.

The steam hissed and the cooling metal clicked intermittently as the heat dissipated. The hideously contorted, blackened figure slumped forward, its black talons melted to the remains of the steering wheel, the cloying smell of burnt flesh mixed with the harsh acidic smell of melted plastic.

After the fire was successfully dealt with, the wreckage was left for the investigators and the police to take over.

Later, on the way back to the station, one of the firefighters said to Greg, 'You think you know the guy?'

Greg was obviously in some distress. 'Oh God, I don't know how Kirsty and her parents are going to take this.'

'You mean Kirsty in the station?'

'Yes, it's her brother.'

'How can you be so sure? The victim has been burnt to a crisp.'

'I saw the number plate. It's Johnny's car, all right, and no way would he ever allow anyone else to drive it. Kirsty and her mother have always doted on him. I don't know how I'm going to tell them.'

'I suppose it would be better coming from you than anyone else.'

'I know. I know. Kirsty'll be off duty by now so I'll go around to her house as soon as I get back.'

They had already arranged that he would call for her and walk through the gardens with her to his place. She was going to make a meal for them both. Then, after enjoying the meal and a couple of glasses of wine, they would make love.

That wouldn't happen now, of course. He would stay with her and her mother at Botanic Crescent as long as they needed him. He would try his best to be of some comfort and support. Johnny Price had never been his favourite person, to say the least, but he wouldn't have wished such a horrific fate on him. He certainly would never have wanted anything like this to happen for the sake of Kirsty and her mother. He didn't know how Simon Price would react. He never seemed to think much of Johnny, but he was his son. He was bound to have some feeling at the terrible news.

Eventually Greg forced his feet along Queen Margaret Drive and round to Botanic Crescent. He rang the bell of the house at the end of the terrace that had become so pleasantly familiar to him. He had never thought he would feel it such an ordeal to wait for the door to open.

Kirsty welcomed him with a kiss, happy and smiling at first, until she noticed how serious his face was.

'Darling, is there something wrong?'

They had reached the sitting room and he put an arm around her and led her to a seat.

'Bad news, I'm afraid, Kirsty. You'll have to try and be brave for your mother's sake.'

'Is it something about Johnny?' she cried out. 'Has something happened to Johnny?'

He might have known that any bad news in the Price family was always connected with Johnny, and so Kirsty would know immediately. Not the horrific details, of course.

'Darling,' he said gently, 'there's been a car accident.' He went over and gathered her up into his arms. 'Johnny didn't survive it.'

'Johnny's dead?'

'Yes. I was on one of the engines that attended the accident. He was the only one in the car . . .'

'But are you sure . . .'

'Yes, darling. To everyone else it was a case of the victim being unrecognisable. But there's absolutely no doubt in my mind, darling, it was Johnny at the wheel. You know how proud he was of that car. He'd never let anyone else drive it.'

She began to weep and moan.

'Oh Johnny. Poor Johnny. He had such a difficult life. So much pain when he was a child and a teenager. He was only recently getting over all that. Oh Greg, how am I going to tell my mother? She loved him so much. She'll be absolutely broken-hearted. It might even kill her. Oh Greg, I can't bear it.'

He held her tightly and tried his best to soothe her.

Eventually he said, 'Do you want me to tell her?'

'No, I'm the one who should talk to her, but stay with me, please.'

'Of course, darling. For as long as you like. Is your father in? He's got to be told too.'

Her voice turned bitter. 'Oh, he's out drinking as usual. No doubt with some of his adoring fans. I can't imagine him being broken-hearted when he hears that Johnny's dead. He never had a good word to say about him.'

'I think a lot of it is just his manner. He's bound to have felt something for his son.'

Secretly Greg could understand Simon Price's attitude. He could never have thought of a good word to say about Johnny Price himself. He had caused nothing but worry to Kirsty, and now the worry had been replaced by terrible grief.

# 21

So far, so good. Betty Powell kept mentally rubbing her hands in glee. Her mother was still in hospital and couldn't talk. She prayed that the miserable, domineering old bitch would be silent for ever. Meantime, for the first time in her life, she was experiencing true freedom. She could get up when she wanted, go to bed when she wanted, eat what she wanted, drink what she wanted. She discarded the woollen cardigan her mother had bought her for a denim jacket and trousers instead. She even had a stylish short haircut. For the first time in her life, she bought and wore make-up. Not too much – just a little blusher and a touch of lipstick to give her pale face some colour, to liven it up a bit. She admired her appearance in the bedroom mirror and was hugely delighted. She looked a new woman. The next step was to return to the Art School. She had a lot of work to do before the show. It was quite a while away yet, but she would need the time to finish all the work she was supposed to include.

At the Art School show, everyone's work would be displayed. Joiners and other workmen came and set up tables and shelves all over the place. Then paintings, sculptures, needlework, metalwork, stained glass, pottery – every aspect of the wonderful variety of art taught at the School – would be displayed. Then it would be judged and a notice would go up listing all the students and next to their names would be either a pass, or a failure to gain their degree.

Students always crowded round the board in an agony of suspense.

She told herself that she didn't care whether she passed or failed. She could get a job somewhere, anywhere. Life had become a great adventure. But in truth, she had to admit she would prefer a pass. A degree would be something to be proud of and necessary to qualify her for a job as an art teacher, for instance. More than that, though, it would be such a terrific boost to her self-confidence and self-worth.

If she went back to the School now and worked hard, she could have enough to put in the show. She could just imagine her still life, her life modelling, all her paintings and other artwork proudly on display and crowds of people milling about admiring it, buying it even. The show was open to the public and was always well attended. Before it was opened to the public, of course, the relief at finishing the course and all the hard work it entailed was expressed in such a wild and reckless show of joy and celebration that the street had to be closed off to the public for their safety on the day the course finished.

Betty kept thinking about it and looking forward to it. She'd never bothered to think about it before. It would have been pointless. Because of the fear of her mother finding out about what she did at the School, she would have had to stay away and keep quiet about it.

Now, it was the danger of her mother recovering and returning home that she tried not to think about. If her mother's voice recovered and she returned home, she would rage on endlessly at Betty. Her mother would never forgive her. Never in a million years.

'You wicked creature!' She could just imagine her mother saying it. 'You will burn in hell for ever. You're disgusting, an absolute disgrace.' It would go on. And on. And on.

But then her new-found sensations of happiness and freedom would surge over her and she'd think, 'Why should I care? Why should I even listen to her? I could just walk away, into another room, or leave the house and go to a cinema or to a café for a cup of coffee and some younger company.' She didn't even need to go straight home after her day at the Art School. She could go with the others to the CCA, where there was a nice café. Or even to one of the clubs she knew the others frequented.

Betty had always avoided even speaking to the others before. She'd felt it was pointless. She had felt so hopeless, guilty, intimidated and depressed. Now everything was different. They had always been friendly. It had been her own fault that they'd given up talking to her or bothering about her eventually. She felt sure that if she made the effort to be friendly now, they would respond.

She had behaved badly in other ways too, of course, and she deeply regretted her actions, especially about trying to cause a fire and stalking Greg. She wasn't quite so sure that side of her behaviour would be so easily forgotten or forgiven.

But her fellow students were a good crowd, and if they saw that she was a changed character, hopefully they would understand and give her another chance.

Anyway, she couldn't stay away from the School for ever. It was high time she returned to work and faced the music, whatever that might be.

As it turned out, everyone was surprisingly sympathetic.

'How is your mother now, Betty? Is there any improvement?'

She explained about how her mother was still in hospital and how she'd lost the power of speech. She'd even said, 'Thank goodness for that in a way. She was always nagging me and telling me what I had to do. When she does manage to talk again, I'll never hear the end of how wicked I am, being in this class. She'll tell me I'll be going right down to burn in hell.'

They all laughed then. But it was kindly, sympathetic laughter. Hamish Ferguson said, 'Gosh, Betty. She sounds even worse than my mother.'

Everything was all right after all. They chatted to her and she chatted to them. Perhaps a little too much at first, in her excitement at being able to talk at all. They didn't seem to mind.

She went with them to the rec at break time and didn't even feel unhappy or jealous about Sandra Matheson and Tommy Pratt looking so much in love. Though Tommy didn't look so happy now. Indeed, he looked as hopeless and depressed as she used to feel. She teetered on the verge of speaking to him about it. Just in the nick of time, she controlled the urge. After all, it was none of her business. Tommy had Sandra to speak to him about whatever was bothering him and Sandra obviously cared about him.

But she wished Tommy well. Nobody, but nobody, should go through what she had gone through.

She knew it wasn't going to be easy but she was determined that she was not going to go through it all again. She was free. She had a life now and she was going to live it.

# 22

Simon Price had to half-carry his wife to the funeral. They had all told her that she was not fit to attend, but she had tearfully insisted. 'I have to say my last goodbye to my dear and loving son.'

It was a very moving service conducted by the Reverend Peter Gordon, and afterwards they returned to Botanic Crescent for a buffet meal that Kirsty had prepared beforehand. Now Sandra helped by putting the kettle on and making a pot of tea. It had been a small gathering with the family, Greg, Tommy and Sandra, and Paul and Renee. A few of Johnny's young Goth friends had turned up at the church but had declined an invitation to come back to the house for tea.

'We'd rather toast Johnny's memory in his local,' they said before slouching away.

Mrs Price still refused to go to bed for a rest. Kirsty could understand it in a way. It was safer to remain in the company of friends and family for as long as possible, rather than be alone with her grief. Once alone, it could become unbearable. Kirsty was dreading it herself. Greg was on night duty and had to leave immediately after the meal, but he promised to return to see her early the next day. She was taking one or two mornings off work and so wouldn't see him at the station. After tomorrow, though, she had to at least think of returning to work. Her mother assured her that she would be all right after that.

Of course, they both knew that neither of them would ever get over their grief. It would only become more manageable as time passed. Now they chatted in an almost normal, even cheerful way, over the meal. They tried their best to hang on to the company of the others for as long as possible, both secretly dreading being on their own when bedtime came. Kirsty would be alone. At least her mother had her father, but in another single bed, and the two beds were separated by a large chest of drawers. Anyway, her mother knew only too well how critical he had always been of Johnny. She could just imagine him believing the accident had been Johnny's own fault. But he had the decency not to say so – so far.

To all appearances, her father had tried to be supportive of her mother. Kirsty had been sarcastic and bitter to Greg about this but he didn't understand.

'Darling, Johnny was his son. He's bound to be suffering . . .'

'Suffering?' she echoed. 'He never had a good word to say about Johnny. He never cared about him.'

'Now, you don't know that, Kirsty. Some people just can't show emotion. Men are especially bad at that. But it doesn't mean they don't have any feelings.'

How ironic, she thought.

When Johnny was alive, she and Greg had argued about him. Now that he was dead, they were arguing about her father. Her father's talent as an artist, of course, gained him many friends and much forgiveness and understanding.

'You know what he's like. You've heard how nasty he can be to the students, especially Tommy, in the Art School.'

'OK. I wouldn't allow him to speak to me the way he speaks to the students, but I suspect he's just trying to get them to do their best and gain their degree. He was all right to Tommy today.'

'Oh yes, he was very charming today. He can be charming when he likes.'

'I'll have to go, Kirsty. Promise me you'll take one of the sedatives the doctor gave your mother, and go to bed as soon as the others leave. After a good night's sleep, you'll feel better.'

She swallowed down a sarcastic retort and she even managed a smile.

'All right, darling. I'll see you tomorrow.'

'Yes, I'll come over before I start my shift. OK?'

She nodded, then saw him to the door. He strode away along the Crescent and round into Queen Margaret Drive. She shut the door and took a deep breath before returning to the sitting room.

Later, Sandra and Tommy helped her to clear up, and wash and dry the dishes. By this time, her father had persuaded her mother to go to bed. He said goodnight and retired with her. Then, when Sandra and Tommy left, Kirsty switched off all the lights and was just about to go up to bed in her own room, when she heard the cat's bell. It came from the back of the house. She returned to the kitchen, and through the shadows she saw Jingles weaving backwards and forwards at the back door. It obviously wanted out.

She opened the door slightly. Then she immediately staggered back in shock. She thought she was going to faint. She hadn't even enough strength to scream.

Her brother Johnny was standing in the doorway.

# 23

'Come on, Betty.'

They were all going to the rec for a break. Betty smiled and called over, 'Right.'

She was still a bit shy and unable to talk with the same ease as the others but she felt such thankfulness and happiness that they hadn't given up on her and she could go along with them and eagerly listen to everyone. Sometimes she would burst out with something and, as often as not, it would make them laugh. They were laughing at her but she didn't mind. It was friendly laughter.

She still lusted after Greg McFarlane, but sadly, when he was there, he either glanced at her with dislike or ignored her altogether.

She had a terrible struggle with herself not to follow him or watch him anywhere outside of the Art School. She tried her best to look attractive in the hope that she might see a glimmer of admiration in his eyes. She now wore a short denim skirt and a low-necked top, and even lipstick, but nothing made a bit of difference. She lived for the days when he was the art model and she could devour his body with her eyes. She was at least rewarded by the tutor.

'Good,' he said, standing back and staring at her painting. 'Yes, you've captured something there.'

Love. That's what she had captured. Her love for Greg McFarlane. It was in every careful brush stroke. Hope was fizzling out, though. Greg McFarlane had a girlfriend. Betty heard all about her from the conversations of the other students. Her name was Kirsty Price, and she was the daughter of the tutor, of all people. Kirsty and Greg were going to get married and it was obviously with the blessing of Simon Price. He always chatted in a very friendly manner to Greg, indeed seemed to have great admiration for him. Who wouldn't admire such a man, of course? Betty struggled to banish him from her mind when he wasn't sitting as a model in front of her. But it was a losing battle. She fantasised about him. She wrote poetry about him. He filled her sleeping hours with erotic dreams. She told herself that it was all a waste of time. He belonged to someone else. She was being stupid and ridiculous. She knew it. Yet she couldn't stop her wayward thoughts. She would still be stalking Greg, had it not been for Tommy and Sandra's strong warnings. No way could she risk being banished from the Glasgow School of Art. Apart from anything else, it had always been her blessed escape from her mother.

She tried to concentrate on her work and to look forward to the preparations for the eventual Degree Show. It would be wonderful if she got her degree. Then she could take a teaching course, and would be qualified to teach art herself. She could start a career as a teacher in one of Glasgow's schools. Or even in a school further afield. She would be paid a wage and would be independent. That thought certainly made her feel happy.

Of course, her mother still had to be reckoned with. Every time Betty visited the hospital, there was her mother propped up in bed, hair straggling down each side of her face, eyes burning with hatred, sunk deep into the dark cavities of her face. She had not yet recovered her power of speech, perhaps never would. Now that would be a blessing, Betty thought. She could just imagine the tirade of vicious abuse that she would be subjected to, if her mother's voice did return.

'You wicked, wicked girl. God will punish you. You will burn forever in hell. You are a wicked, wicked liar, a disgusting, revolting . . .' And so it would go on, and on. And on.

If her mother did recover her voice, Betty would have to find a way of shutting her up again. They were beginning to say in hospital that her mother might get on better and be happier and more content if she was at home. When had her mother ever been happy or content? Well, maybe she was happy in some twisted way, gossiping with one of the neighbours who was as malicious and narrow-minded as herself. They talked about all the 'wicked young people' that they viewed from their windows or read about in the papers. Her mother was content with the repetitive structure of her life.

'But I'm not,' Betty thought. Of that she was very certain. No way was she going back to any of her mother's excruciatingly boring routines.

Then the last time she visited the hospital, her mother was up and dressed and sitting on a chair beside the bed. The nurse said, 'Isn't she doing well? You must be pleased. She's eating well and that's building up her strength. She hasn't recovered her voice but, given time, that could happen too. Let's hope so anyway.'

Betty didn't hope anything of the kind. It was depressing enough to see her mother looking more or less back to normal. Even her hair had been neatly pinned back into its customary bun at the nape of her neck.

'She'll be able to go home any time now.'

'Oh God!' Betty thought.

She wondered what her mother's reaction would be to the changes in the house. Her beloved cake stand had gone. And her precious china tea set. The silver teapot had been donated to Oxfam, along with the embroidered tea cloths and linen napkins.

Mugs decorated with funny words or pictures had replaced the floral tea set. Paper serviettes were handier than the linen ones. They didn't need washed and ironed. Nor did the plastic cover for the table.

Her mother would not be happy either when she discovered that Betty had used up so much of the money her mother kept around the house – in the biscuit barrel, in the kitchen-table drawer, in the velvet-lined box on her bedside table. It was one of her mother's eccentricities. There was even money in a suitcase under the bed. Her mother didn't trust banks or building societies.

'Please God, don't let her get her voice back,' Betty kept thinking. Her looks of fury and hatred would be bad enough.

Meantime, Betty made the most of her freedom inside the house and outside of it. She went to a club with the other students. She went to a pub and stood at the bar and ordered a round of drinks for her friends. What a lovely thought that was. She had friends. She included a large bottle of cider for herself and enjoyed drinking it down. It made her feel good, increased her sense of freedom.

Let her mother do her worst. She didn't care any more.

# 24

Kirsty staggered back until she crashed violently against the kitchen table, making her cry out in pain. Dazed, she grabbed at the table to steady herself.

'Kirsty, it's me, it's me.' The wind snatched the voice and squeezed it into a whisper before the silhouetted figure in the doorway darted into the house.

Eyes strained with horrified disbelief, Kirsty watched white fingers lock the kitchen door and bolt it.

She shrank back, screwing her eyes tightly shut. Surely she was having a nightmare. Hadn't she been very overwrought? The shock of Johnny's death, the strain of his funeral and worry about her mother had played havoc with her nerves. Was it any wonder she had nightmares? But everything was quiet again. If she opened her eyes now, she would gaze through soft shadows at the familiar surroundings of her bedroom. There was nothing to be afraid of.

Cautiously she relaxed the tense muscles of her eyes, but through a shimmery veil of lashes, she still saw the same grey face.

'Kirsty, it's me. Johnny.'

'But you're . . . You're . . .' Kirsty's tongue refused to form the word.

'Dead?' He said it for her. 'No, I'm very much alive and just as scared as you are.'

His delicate skin gleamed grey-white, his eyes stretched huge and he was trembling. Immediately all the pity and protective love she'd always felt for her brother came rushing back.

'Johnny!' Her arms had barely stretched out for him when he stumbled weeping against her.

'I'm sorry.' His young voice broke and his tears mingled with her own. 'Please forgive me. I had to come.'

'But Johnny, I don't understand.' She pushed him back so that she could have another look at him. 'If you're not dead, who was the dead man found in your car?'

'I can explain.' His hands fumbled for a handkerchief and his eyes sought to avoid hers.

'Sit down, Johnny. Over there by the fire. I'll make you a hot cup of tea while you tell me. But we'll have to be very quiet. If Mum heard you or saw you, she'd die of shock. I feel pretty shocked myself but I'm thankful you're alive and well.'

Johnny flashed her a tragic look. 'I wouldn't be too sure.'

'What do you mean?'

'Maybe it would have been better if I had died.'

'Johnny, what nonsense . . .'

'Anyway, I will if you don't help me.'

'Will what?'

'Die.' His ashen face tipped pathetically towards her. 'I'll die in prison, Kirsty.'

'Johnny, why are you talking like this?' She went over to make the tea, all the time fighting back tears of distress.

'I don't understand. What's happened?'

'Well, it was Paul's idea to begin with . . .'

'I might have known.' She groaned. 'Johnny, why do you allow yourself to be so easily influenced by people, especially people like Paul and Renee?'

'Paul's OK,' Johnny assured her hastily. 'It wasn't his fault that everything went wrong. No, Kirsty, you're making a mistake about him. He's doing his darnedest to help me. He got me here today, for instance. He hid me in the boot of his car and drove down here on the pretext of coming to the funeral.'

'But he left hours ago with Renee. Where have you been since then?'

'Hiding in the tool shed waiting for your firefighter man to leave. I knew I daren't move a muscle while he was around.'

Suddenly Kirsty felt icy cold.

'What was Paul's idea to begin with?'

'You know how he's a croupier in a gambling club?' A flush crept up from Johnny's neck. 'And . . . and you see . . . they draw in a lot of money there. Real big money – thousands and thousands of pounds. The manager always goes to the bank with it on the same day every week. Regular as clockwork, Paul said. So . . . you see . . . that meant that the night before, the safe in the manager's office is always crammed full. Just asking to be lifted, Paul said.'

Kirsty slumped down on one of the chairs. 'Johnny, how could you . . .'

'Well, Paul said it wasn't as if it was the manager's money, you see. The club belongs to a big company. They own a string of places all over Britain. And Paul said they wouldn't miss it because they are so well insured.'

'Paul said . . . Paul said . . .' Kirsty repeated brokenly. 'Must you always do everything Paul says? Don't you know right from wrong? Haven't you a mind of your own at all, Johnny?'

'Yes, but I couldn't help thinking of what I could do with all that money, Kirsty. Paul said it would be easy, you see. He'd even managed to get a copy of the safe key and we were to go fifty-fifty with everything in it. I was just to step into the manager's office by the lane window that Paul had left unlocked. The manager eats supper at the club dining room at the same time every night. He takes a book and reads it while he's eating. Paul and Renee both said they'd keep an eye on the dining-room door from their roulette tables. Not that Paul expected the manager to return to his office in much less than an hour. Why should he?' Johnny's mouth twisted. 'He's never done it before. But of course, as Paul said, this time, of all times, the man had to leave his spectacles on the office desk and he came straight back for them. I was bending down in front of the safe. I'd just stuffed the money into a bag . . .' His voice cracked and he suddenly buried his face in his hands. 'Kirsty, it was awful. I'll never forget it as long as I live. Never.

'I tried to run away, Kirsty. I was so frightened. But he wouldn't let me go. He grabbed me. I struggled to push him away but he was stronger than me. Then I remembered . . . I remembered . . .' He stopped, his eyes anguished.

'What?'

'The gun. Oh, I'd no intention of using it. Such a terrible thought never entered my head. Paul didn't want me to use it. "It'll just help give you enough courage," he said. "Make you feel ten feet tall." He knew I was scared, you see.'

'Johnny . . .' Helpless with despair, Kirsty shook her head.

'I didn't want to use it, but when the manager tried to stop me getting away, I pulled it out on the spur of the moment, just to frighten him into leaving me alone.' Tears glistened over his eyes. 'I couldn't allow him to phone the police. I suddenly thought of Mum and what all this would do to her. I told him to get back. I pushed him back. All I wanted was to get away. But he lunged at me again. Then before I knew what had happened, he was on the ground at my feet, blood oozing from his head.'

'Johnny, no . . .'

'I didn't mean to kill him, Kirsty.' Johnny began to shiver as if he'd caught a violent chill. He clutched at himself, hugging his shoulders, shaking and rocking himself to and fro. 'I didn't mean to kill him. But there he was . . . lying there . . . so still. I nearly went out of my mind. I just stood there until Renee came in to see what had happened because they'd seen the manager go back into the office. But she said it would be all right. They would arrange everything.'

'What do you mean, arrange everything?' Kirsty cried out distractedly.

'The car accident. Paul rigged it. He said it was a foolproof method of getting away with both the robbery and the murder. He said the police would find an empty safe and no manager and come to the obvious conclusion that he'd hopped it with the cash. Then later, the local police would find an accident involving a local boy who'd been warned more than once about driving too fast and under the influence. Nothing to make them suspicious there.'

'You mean the charred body in your car . . .'

'Yes.' Johnny's childish blue eyes clung desperately to hers. 'It was the manager's body.'

'Oh, Johnny.' She stared back at him with a desperation matching his.

'Hide me just now, Kirsty,' he pleaded. 'Oh please.'

'But Johnny, how can I?'

'Kirsty, please.' Hysteria leapt suddenly into his voice. 'You've got to, just until Paul arranges to get me safely out of the country. We're all going abroad. Paul and Renee and me. Paul's arranging it.'

'Johnny, if it hadn't been for that man, you wouldn't be in all this terrible trouble. He wasn't to be trusted at the beginning and he's not to be trusted now.'

'He'll arrange everything all right, Kirsty. I've made sure he will. I've still got the money and the gun, you see.'

He jerked open his loose-fitting coat to reveal a big canvas bag strapped around his waist.

'This was made specially for the job. Renee took a lot of trouble with it. If I'd been seen by a policeman walking from that lane at the club carrying a case or a bag, he might have been suspicious and asked me to open it. They can do that, you know. But if I just strolled out from the lane with my hands in my pockets, the chances are nothing would have been said. Of course, nobody saw me. It had been arranged that I'd get back out through the window and I still had to do that, as quick as I could. Paul and Renee had to hurry back to their tables so that they wouldn't be suspected. Paul said I had to take the money away. The money was too hot for him to touch. He's safer without it just now. I know he's right but I'm so terribly afraid, I just can't bear to take any chances. See . . .' He plunged his hand into the inside pocket of his coat. 'I've got the gun here too.'

'Put it away. I don't want to see it,' Kirsty cried. 'And I don't want anything to do with that money either.'

'But Kirsty, there's thousands and thousands of pounds here. After I'm safely abroad and all the fuss has blown over, I'll send you some, enough for you and Mum to come and join me.'

'Will you never learn? How can you expect to get any happiness with that money? Look what it's done to you already.'

'I've no choice but to keep it and use it now.'

'Yes, you have. You can give it to the police and tell them what you've just told me. Surely it would go in your favour . . .'

'They'd take me away and put me in prison for life. You know they would. Oh, Kirsty, you can't let them do that, not you.' Tears brimmed over and trickled helplessly down his face. 'Kirsty, I'm frightened.'

Impulsively, she took him in her arms to comfort and reassure him. So often in the past, when he was a child, she'd done this, and he was a child again now.

'Please help me.' He clung to her, weeping.

'It's all right. Don't worry. I won't allow anyone to hurt you. Calm down now and drink your tea. I'll think of something.'

Her heart told her she'd no choice but to help protect her young brother. After all, he hadn't meant to kill anyone. It was all a ghastly mistake, a tragic accident.

At the same time, she'd no idea how she could possibly hide Johnny in the house without her mother seeing or hearing him.

Her mother's life could be at stake now, as well as Johnny's. Her own life too, in a way, because Greg must never know. He had never liked Johnny at the best of times. If Greg found out, he would immediately march Johnny to the police station. She had no doubt whatever about that.

# 25

Betty groaned to herself. There was no escaping it. She had to take her mother home. The nurse said that although her voice had not returned and there was a weakness down one side which affected her arm and leg, Mrs Powell was fit enough to go home.

'It'll take her a little time to get used to balancing herself with her stick,' the nurse explained to Betty. 'And you'll have to help her to get around at first but let's hope she'll make a full recovery eventually.'

Betty lifted her mother's case and linked arms with her. Her mother jerked away but staggered as a result. The nurse smiled at Betty.

'She's so independent, isn't she?' Then to the older woman, 'Now, you've got to be patient and accept help from your daughter, Mrs Powell. You're not able to walk perfectly on your own just yet.'

Betty took her mother's arm again and felt resentment stiffen through it. This time, however, her mother allowed herself to be led away. They took a taxi home. It was when they came to the close in Great Western Road that it became very difficult. Their flat was up a flight of stairs and it took all Betty's strength to heave her mother up each step until they reached the Powell front door. Betty propped her mother against the wall at the side of the door until she found the key in her pocket and slid it into the lock.

'I'll get you comfortably settled in your chair, Mother, and then I'll make us a cup of tea.'

There was no mistaking the horror in her mother's eyes as she stared at the table set for tea. Her eyes took in the plastic tablecloth, the wooden plate that held the chocolate cream biscuits, the mugs, the cheap glass milk jug and sugar dish. Then the plastic stay-hot teapot that didn't need a tea cosy.

Just in time, Betty dodged a blow from her mother's stick. She grabbed the stick and wrenched it from her mother's hand. For a second, she felt like crashing it over the older woman's head. But she resisted the temptation. She was glad she did. It proved to her that she was her own woman now, and she was not going to be a victim any more, either of her mother or of her own over-intense emotions.

'Now, Mother, we'll have none of that nonsense. Just try to calm down and accept things as they are now. You've had many, many years of everything being how you wanted it. Now it's my turn. It's only fair.'

She poured the tea, added milk and sugar, and put one of the mugs in front of her mother.

'Have one of these chocolate creams. They're really very nice.'

With a sweep of her good hand, Mrs Powell sent all of the biscuits on the wooden platter flying to the floor.

Quietly Betty picked them up and replaced them on the platter, but made sure that this time it was out of her mother's reach.

'All right then. You won't have anything to eat just now. I'll be cooking a meal later on. If you don't eat that, you'll just have to go to bed hungry.' She took a few sips of tea. 'Tomorrow I have to go to the Art School. But I'll make you a good breakfast before I go and I'll leave you something for lunch. I'm sometimes late getting back. But that should keep you going. If you need anything extra, there's packets of sandwiches in the fridge. Micro chips in the freezer if you fancy them, as well.'

Her mother lifted the mug of tea that Betty had given her and poured it all over the table. It overflowed down onto the carpet.

Betty willed herself to keep calm. No way was her mother going to have any effect on her ever again. No way was she going to ruin her life or her personality ever again.

She sighed. 'All right, Mother. I'll just enjoy my tea on my own. You're only punishing yourself, you know. I don't care any more what you do or what you think of me.'

It took all of her willpower, however, to sit to all appearances coolly enjoying her mug of tea while her mother's glare of hatred burned into her face. She managed it, though. Then she cleared the table and mopped up the spilled tea.

'You'll have noticed,' she said, 'that I've bought a television. I'm going to switch it on so that you can watch the news. I'll leave it on because you might enjoy *Coronation Street*, and I think there's a police series after that. You must have got quite used to television in hospital. I saw there was one in the ward. I've got to go back to the Art School now but I'll try not to be too late tonight.'

Betty didn't really need to go back to the Art School for the afternoon tutorials, but she just could not face sitting opposite her mother for the rest of the day and evening. First, though, she went through to the bedroom and wheeled a commode back to the sitting room, and positioned it next to her mother's chair.

'I know you'd probably manage to the bathroom with the help of your stick, but until you get more used to walking with it on your own, you'd better use the commode.'

After washing the mugs, Betty left a couple of slices of

smoked salmon and a sliced tomato on a plate. If hunger overcame her mother, she'd no doubt manage to get to the kitchen and eat the salmon. It would be her own fault if she remained hungry. She had thought of setting it out on the table in the sitting room, but probably her mother would just throw it at her. No, if her mother wanted anything now while Betty was at the Art School, she would have to hobble through to the kitchen.

It was such a relief once she got there and joined the other students. They all stopped to ask about what happened and she told them truthfully and exactly what did happen.

'Oh God, Betty. How on earth can you go on putting up with that?'

Betty shrugged. 'I'm hoping she'll give up gracefully. I doubt it, but you never know. At least I can escape and come here every day. At least until the show. After that, I don't know what I'll do.'

Sandra said, 'Oh surely she'll have learned to behave herself by then. The show isn't for a wee while yet.'

'Where's Mr Price, by the way?'

'Oh, he's down at some art festival in England, thank goodness. I hope they keep him there for a while and give my Tommy a rest.' She lowered her voice. 'I'm getting seriously worried about him.'

'I can understand how he feels,' Betty sympathised. 'I've gone through depression and all sorts of negative moods, as you know, and I wouldn't wish any of that on my worst enemy.'

They both looked over at where Tommy was sitting at his easel, shoulders hunched, staring miserably at his canvas.

'He's so talented as well,' Sandra whispered.

'Yes, I know. He's as good as Price, if not even better.'

'He is, isn't he?' Sandra agreed triumphantly. 'I keep telling him that but it never makes a bit of difference. He thinks it's just me. He thinks I just say things like that to please him and cheer him up. He never believes me. Never for a minute. And it's so true about his talent, isn't it?'

'Of course. We all think so.'

'I'll try and get him out for a drink after we finish here tonight. Maybe everyone will come with us. At least that way he won't get to sit alone and feel sorry for himself.'

'I'll come anyway and I'm sure everyone else will too.'

'But what about your mother?'

'Oh, I've no doubt she'll manage. It's only her voice and a bit of weakness down one side, and she's got her stick for that.'

'Well, it's kind of you, Betty. I really appreciate your support.'

Betty felt like hugging Sandra. It was so wonderful to have friends. Their affection towards her more than made up for her mother's lack of any. She would have to avoid going back to Great Western Road and her mother for as long as possible, of course. She always used to dread it. Now she dreaded it again.

# 26

'I could hide in the loft, couldn't I, Kirsty? No one would hear me and no one would have any reason to come up there. You'd have no need to worry.'

No need to worry? The words cavorted crazily in Kirsty's brain. She'd have plenty to worry about, all right. 'The loft's the safest place, I suppose, but you couldn't stay there for long.'

'It wouldn't be for long, I promise.'

'It's so cramped and cold and you're not strong at the best of times, Johnny. You'd be sure to catch pneumonia, or worse.'

'I'll be fine. You'll see. Paul will have everything fixed in no time.'

But why was this man doing so much for Johnny? There could only be one answer – the stolen money. That was all Paul cared about. Kirsty felt certain of it.

'How is he going to get you out of the country?'

'He's got lots of contacts, Kirsty, with officers and crews from all sorts of ships that dock down the Clyde. They regularly visit the casino and loads of them owe Paul favours.'

'Tell Paul you must go first, and alone, Johnny. Then see what he says.'

'All right. I could give him his share of the money once I'm safely aboard the ship. Or tell him where he could find it. I could leave it hidden here if you want. That way you'd have nothing to worry about.'

'Paul could take all the money beforehand and just leave you here.'

'No, he wouldn't, Kirsty. He's not like that. Anyway, he knows as well as I do that I can't stay hidden in this house for ever, and if I'm found, everything'll be discovered, including the part Paul played in all this. After all, he's an accessory to murder. He's in it up to his neck too. No, Kirsty, I'm supposed to be dead, and as long as everyone believes I'm dead, I'm safe, and Paul is in the clear.'

Kirsty already had a blinding headache with fear and worry. She scarcely knew what she was thinking or saying any more. She screwed up her face, straining her eyes as if trying to see straight.

'I don't like that man, Johnny. There's something about him. He makes me feel frightened. I can't bring myself to trust him.'

'He's all right, Kirsty. Honestly.'

'Oh, what do you know? You're so naive. You've always been the same, Johnny. You've always been far too impressionable, far too easily taken in.'

A miserable flush suffused Johnny's face. 'I'm sorry, Kirsty. I'll do whatever you say. Just tell me.'

Kirsty sighed. 'I think you'd be a lot safer if you took that money bag off and hid it. Somewhere Paul wouldn't know about.'

'All right, Kirsty.' He jumped up, struggling to unstrap the bag from his waist, only too eager to please her. 'I'll hide it now. But where do you think I should put it?' His big eyes anxiously roamed around the room. 'It's so risky, isn't it, because Greg comes here.'

The mere mention of Greg's name caused Kirsty's heart to pound and it was only with great difficulty that she said, 'No, not here. Upstairs in my bedroom would be safest. I'll show you. But quietly, Johnny, for pity's sake. Don't even breathe when you're passing Mum's room.'

Hand in hand, they ventured into the hall, their heads close, their eyes riveted on their mother's door.

The sleepy quiet of the night enveloped the house. Outside the wind howled mournfully. They listened, as with painful caution they eased towards the stairs.

How she survived the night, Kirsty didn't know. She'd been exhausted before it began but by the time she got rid of some of the dust in the loft, made up a camp bed for Johnny and carried up all the things she thought he might need, she was on the point of collapsing. Yet when she finally did crumple into bed, she could not sleep.

Never before in her life had she felt so frightened. If only she could confide in Greg. If only he could do something. She daren't say one word to him, though. She knew how he felt about Johnny. She also knew his close police connections. Thinking of Johnny huddled upstairs in the cold and airless loft made tears gush to her eyes.

He was alone. He was frightened too. Come what may, she had to try her very best to help and protect him.

In the loft, the hatch had clicked shut with frightening finality. The loft space seemed diminished and more threatening somehow. The camping light cast a small pool of golden light around Johnny's feet. The roof beams cast looming shadows and he sat shivering with cold and nerves, his mind racing over and over the events of the last few days. It was all one terrible nightmare.

He sat, knees tucked into chest, as time slowly ebbed by. He started every now and then as some tiny rustle or creak took on ominous dimensions in his overwrought mind. He looked at his watch and the hands slowly, so slowly, marked the passing time.

Kirsty arose after dozing fitfully for two or three hours, and on her way downstairs to make breakfast her eyes strayed towards the ceiling. There was no sign of movement. Anxiety made her heart beat a little faster. She prayed that Johnny was all right. He had looked so over-strained, so feverishly excited. She decided to make a flask of coffee and take it up to the loft with a breakfast tray, before going near her mother's room to waken her.

It was when she was tiptoeing upstairs with the loaded tray that she realised what a problem it was going to be getting food regularly to Johnny. Early morning, or late at night, would probably be the only safe times. Greg dropped in whenever he could and that, it suddenly occurred to Kirsty, was going to prove both nerve-racking and dangerous.

'Johnny,' she whispered, as she lowered the folding stairs by which the small entrance to the loft was reached. 'Johnny, are you there?'

Awkwardly she climbed the stairs, while at the same time clutching the tray in one hand. She thought she heard a scuffling, scraping sound.

'Johnny,' she repeated softly. 'Open the hatch. Hurry up, I'm carrying something heavy.'

A long minute passed.

'Johnny!'

Slowly the wooden hatch creaked open. Johnny's nervous white face appeared over the opening.

'Take this tray,' Kirsty whispered. 'I've made you a good big breakfast and there's a flask of coffee for later. Johnny, are you all right?'

The hands that pulled the tray up were blue-tinged and trembling. Then they disappeared, leaving just the dark empty hole in the ceiling. Kirsty hoisted herself upwards and clambered into the loft after her brother. It was a big place crowded with junk and too-big furniture and heaped with relics of the past like school books, teddy bears, and schoolboy stamp collections. Early morning light pushed patchily through the frost-covered skylight, under which a space had been cleared for a camp bed and a little basketwork table.

Johnny sat hunched in the bed, a blanket draped round his shoulders.

'I'm cold, Kirsty,' he said brokenly. 'I've never been so cold in all my life.'

She was appalled at the pinched white face and the black circles round his eyes, which looked even bigger than usual.

'Eat your breakfast, love. That'll make you feel better. And there's an old paraffin heater up here somewhere. I'll light it.'

'And you won't tell anyone, will you, Kirsty? You won't let them take me away?'

'No, of course not. Just eat your breakfast and try not to worry.'

'You won't regret helping me, I promise. I'll make it up to you. When I'm safe in another country and you and Mum are living with me, I'll do everything for you and I'll buy you clothes and jewels and . . .'

'It's all right,' Kirsty said gently. 'I'll never regret helping you. I'd better go down and see to Mum now.'

'When will you come back to see me?'

'Just as soon as I can. I'll bring you some books and papers but we'll have to be careful. Greg might come early today because he was worried about leaving Mum and me alone last night after the funeral.'

Johnny struggled up from the bed, still clutching the blanket around his body.

'Oh Kirsty, please don't tell him.'

'Now, now, there's no need for you to get into such a panic. Haven't I promised over and over again that I won't?'

Back downstairs in the kitchen, Kirsty had to feed Jingles the cat first because it kept prowling around her feet, its bell jingling loudly. Then she prepared breakfast for her mother and had no difficulty in persuading her to lie down and sleep again afterwards. The sedatives from the night before had not fully worn off and sleep came easily. 'If only I could sleep too,' Kirsty thought. But she had to see to Johnny's needs.

It was after she'd been to see Johnny again that the front doorbell rang. She stood very still for a moment. Then she took a long, deep breath. Greg would have to be faced sometime. Yet her feet moved slowly and reluctantly across the hall towards the door. She pushed and patted at her hair in an effort to look tidy and normal. But she could feel the cold dampness of perspiration on her face and knew she didn't look her normal, natural self at all.

In sudden desperation, she swung open the door.

'You!' she gasped in shocked surprise when she saw Paul. He was a big man, almost as big as Greg. His blue-black hair was long and sleek, and his skin had a tan reminiscent of sun-soaked beaches and sunbathers on summer holiday posters.

'Aren't you going to invite me in? Kirsty, isn't it?'

'Miss Price,' Kirsty informed him in what she hoped was a cool, firm voice.

'Kirsty,' he repeated and sauntered into the house, his hands jingling coins in his pocket.

'What do you want?' She dropped her voice to a whisper. 'You mustn't come here like this unless it's urgent. My fiancé might see you and then what would he think?'

Paul's eyes glittered round at her. 'Then you'll just have to get rid of him, won't you?'

'I'll do nothing of the kind. I couldn't anyway, even if I wanted to. You don't know my fiancé.'

Paul shrugged. 'That's your problem, beautiful. Where's Johnny?'

'Sh-sh,' Kirsty whispered desperately. 'For pity's sake, remember my mother's sleeping in that room over there. Keep your voice down. Johnny's hiding up in the loft. Why do you want to see him? Have you arranged for a ship already?'

'No, not yet.'

'Then why have you come here today? Why do you want to see Johnny?'

Paul pushed the door shut and looked down at her. 'Maybe I don't want to see Johnny.'

'What do you mean?'

'Maybe I'd rather see his far more attractive sister,' he said.

# 27

Kirsty stood her ground as Paul moved towards her. 'You may not want to see Johnny,' she snapped, 'but he wants to see you. He has something to tell you.'

'Oh?' Paul raised an eyebrow.

'I'll show you the way.'

She pushed past him, secretly sick with anxiety. This man had influenced her brother so much in the past. He was older and more experienced, stronger in every way. It would be easy for him to dominate Johnny again.

'Johnny, don't tell him where the money is,' she repeated fervently to herself all the way up the stairs, praying that in some strange telepathic way the words might reach her brother. 'You mustn't tell him where you've hidden it. You mustn't.'

Kirsty pulled the loft ladder down and beckoned to Paul. 'Up there. But don't be long and for goodness' sake, talk quietly. Remember my mother's in the house and my fiancé is due here at any minute.'

Paul's mouth twisted into a smile as he passed her. 'Don't go away, beautiful. I want to see you again.'

For a minute or two after Paul disappeared inside the loft, Kirsty stood wondering if she should follow him to make sure everything was all right. Eventually she decided to return to the sitting room to watch for Greg. What explanation was she going to give him for Paul's presence in the house? She simply had no idea. In the sitting room, she stared helplessly out of the window, trying to force her mind to find one.

So intent was she in her thoughts that she didn't hear Paul return downstairs and enter the room. His hand unexpectedly on her waist made her gasp and whirl round to face him.

'Don't you dare touch me.'

'I like a girl with nerve, and you've got plenty. I bet you put that brother of yours up to this.'

'Up to what?' Boldly she attempted to stare him out but the fury in his eyes bore into hers with such venom that she was forced to turn away in defeat. 'I don't know what you're talking about.'

'What a beautiful little liar you are.'

His hands grabbed her again and jerked her against him.

'Leave me alone.' She dug clenched fists into his chest and pushed words out through gritted teeth in a desperate effort not to make any noise.

'Let go of me or I'll . . . I'll . . .' She stared up at him, her fury vying with his.

'You'll what?' His grip tightened. 'There's nothing you can do. If you want me to be nice to your precious brother and get him safely aboard a ship real soon, you'll just have to be nice to me, that's all.'

'No, that's not all.'

The angry voice from the doorway made them both spin round in astonishment.

Paul was the first to recover.

'For God's sake, Johnny, get back up to that loft. Her boyfriend is liable to walk in here and find you.'

'Let him.' Johnny's thin face was deathly white and he was trembling, but his voice remained strong and angry. 'It would be worth it to be able to watch what he'd do to you for touching Kirsty.'

'Now look, kid,' Paul laughed softly, 'you can't blame me for trying to make a pass at your sister. She's a very beautiful young woman.'

'Oh, Johnny.' Kirsty ran towards him. 'Don't worry about me. I'll be all right. Just go you back upstairs before Greg comes.'

He put an arm protectively around her shoulders. 'No one is going to hurt you, Kirsty. You know I'd never allow that.' His voice turned bitter. 'I thought he'd try and get his spite out on you. I saw he was angry at me for not telling him where the money is. That's why I came after him.'

'Oh come now . . .' Paul strolled towards them. 'There's no need to be nasty. We're friends, remember. No one's going to get hurt. Unless you, of course, kiddo. When they fling you in a cell in Barlinnie, I mean. They will, you know, if you're not a lot more careful.'

'He's right, Johnny.' Kirsty's gaze flickered anxiously between the sitting-room window and her brother's chalk-white face. 'You can't afford to wander about the house like this. And don't forget, there's Mother to consider as well. She might have seen you. Think of the shock. It would have killed her.'

She glanced out of the large bay window of the living room. Suddenly she gripped his arm. 'He's coming. Johnny, look, there's Greg's car outside. Oh please, hurry back upstairs and don't make a sound. And you . . .' Clutching at Paul's sleeve, she struggled to pull him towards the door. 'Out the back way, quick.'

'Do as she says,' Johnny burst out excitedly. 'Or we'll all have something to worry about, because if you stay, I stay too.'

'OK, OK.'

'Through the kitchen,' Kirsty whispered. 'That's it over there past the stairs. Oh, my goodness . . .' Her hand flew to her mouth. 'Did you bring your car? Have you left it parked in front of the house?'

'I never take chances.' Paul jerked his tie straight, then smoothed it down. 'The car's not near your house.'

The doorbell buzzed loud and long, electrifying all three of them. Paul streaked across the hall and Johnny and Kirsty made for the stairs, their legs trembling so much that they were almost staggering.

Johnny grabbed hold of the banister. 'I'll manage, Kirsty. Just give me a couple of minutes to get out of sight before you open the door.'

She nodded, speechless with distress, as Greg's finger jabbed at the bell once more.

'Kirsty . . .' The sound of her mother's voice barely audible behind the harsh buzz of the bell nearly caused Kirsty to lose consciousness. She leaned dizzily against the banister, for a moment not knowing what to do – go to her mother's room, or let Greg into the house.

Then it occurred to her that if Greg didn't get in through the front door right now, he'd know for certain something must be wrong and he'd dash round to the back of the house and come in through the kitchen. She rushed across the hall and fumbled desperately with the door handle. Greg mustn't bump into Paul.

'Darling . . .' Tears swam in her eyes when she greeted him.

'Kirsty, sweetheart, what's wrong?' His strong arms immediately enfolded her in warmth and comfort.

'Nothing . . . I . . . I . . .' Hastily she rubbed her tears away with the back of her hand. 'I'm just so glad to see you.'

'Is that your mother calling? Has she taken worse or something?'

'I . . . I was just going to see. I don't know.'

Helplessly she gazed up at him. What if her mother had heard voices? Johnny had whispered all the time, but Paul hadn't bothered to keep his voice low. His grey eyes thoughtful, Greg returned her gaze.

'Kirsty, you've had too much to cope with these past few days. You'll be cracking up next. Come on, we'll see to Mum together.'

She had no alternative but to allow him to lead her across the hall and into her mother's room. Mrs Price was struggling to sit up in bed.

'Mum, are you all right?' Kirsty hurried to help her.

'Yes dear, I'm fine. I was beginning to get worried about you, though. What happened? That's the first time you haven't answered when I've called you.'

'But we did, Mum. We both came as soon as we heard you.'

Greg sat down by the bed and patted her hand.

'Oh hello, son.' Mrs Price smiled. 'I see you've still got your coat on. Was it you who was ringing the bell?'

'Guilty, ma'am. Sorry if it wakened you.'

'No, no, it was the voices, son. That's why I called to Kirsty. I wondered what was going on. Then I began to get worried when she didn't answer me, or go to the door when the bell rang.'

'Voices?' Greg flashed Kirsty a questioning look.

Kirsty shook her head. 'It must have been the radio, Mum. I'm terribly sorry I didn't hear you. I'd better not have the sound turned up so loud again.'

'You're not looking well today, Kirsty. It's time I was up and seeing to myself.'

'Nothing's wrong with me, Mum. Except perhaps I'm a little over-tired.'

'Yes, you've been doing far too much, dear. As I say, it's high time I was up out of this bed and looking after you for a change. And I'll start by getting up right now and making the tea.' She smiled. 'But first you'll have to get this big firefighter out of my room.'

'Mum, you can't.'

'And why not, may I ask?'

Greg waggled a finger at her. 'Because I won't let you. I'm making the tea and I don't want any women in my way.'

'You're an awful man. But I've got to get up sometime. And I'll feel better if I can keep busy. I'll be happier getting back to finishing Kirsty's wedding dress.'

'Wait until tomorrow, Mum,' Kirsty pleaded.

'Yes,' Greg agreed. 'Much safer to take things easy. Then by Saturday you'll be able to come to Kirklee Terrace. I'll come first thing in the morning, Kirsty, and you must stay over the weekend this time and let me look after you both. It'll do you good to get out of the house, especially when Simon is away lecturing down south. He doesn't want you to be left here on your own either. He had a word with me earlier.'

'No, it's impossible. I couldn't.' The words flew from Kirsty's lips so quickly that Greg turned to stare at her.

'Why not? What's to prevent you?'

'I've so much to do, Greg.'

'Kirsty, don't be silly, dear,' her mother said. 'I think it's a lovely idea and very kind of Greg. Your dad offered to cancel his course of lectures but I said he mustn't. I told him he mustn't let them down, and we'd be all right, as long as we have Greg to look after us.'

'I can't go,' Kirsty said abruptly. 'It's impossible.'

She turned sharply on her heel and marched through to the kitchen, where she nervously bustled about making tea.

Greg was not to be denied, however. 'Look, Kirsty, I don't see what the problem is. Are you embarrassed about the sleeping arrangements at my flat? Don't worry. I can sleep on the couch. I can control my urges, you know.'

He chuckled, trying to take the reproach from his voice and make light of it.

'All right, all right,' Kirsty gasped eventually. 'Anything to stop you going on and on about it. But just for the day, Greg.'

'Very well.' Greg stared at her curiously. 'I'll bring you and Mum back at night.'

Kirsty took a deep breath. 'I'm sorry if I sound a bit tense and irritable. The strain of the last few days . . .' Her eyes sought his in dumb pleading.

'Don't worry, honey.' He threw her a kiss. 'I understand.'

With excruciating care, she tried to act normally and calmly during the rest of his visit. And she managed with surprising success. Only once did the truth rear up in her mind like a monster.

Here she was calmly chattering with a man who was as honest as the day was long, and who was devoted to saving lives, while at the same time, she was hiding a murderer upstairs.

'I must be mad,' she thought, suddenly teetering between tears and grotesque, sobbing laughter. Pressing her hands over her mouth, she fought for control.

'Kirsty darling, you're far too overwrought.' Greg pulled her against him and pressed her face against his chest. 'I'm going to send Dr Brown to see you. You need a good strong sedative.'

'I'll be all right in a day or two.'

'No, you need help right now. I can't bear to see you like this.'

'He's coming tomorrow to check up on Mum and give her more tablets. I'll speak to him then.'

'Promise?'

'Yes.' She nodded, moist-eyed. 'And I think I'll have an early night tonight. If you don't mind, Greg?'

'I won't mind as long as I get a kiss before I go.' His arms tightened around her and he kissed her with disconcerting passion. 'See you on Saturday, don't forget.'

She nodded. 'Thank you for being so patient and understanding.' She smiled brightly at him. 'But please don't worry. There's really no need.'

She relaxed against the door, sighing with relief when it eventually closed on his straight broad back. Yet at the same time she felt broken-hearted and lonely without him.

It seemed an age until Saturday. She longed to see him and be with him again.

'I'll be fine, Kirsty,' Johnny kept assuring her. 'You go with Mum and have a nice time.'

Johnny worried her, though. He didn't look well and she noticed that his usual slight limp had become rather more pronounced than usual.

'Johnny, is your leg hurting again?' she'd asked. He had suffered with it so much when he'd had rheumatic fever.

'No, honestly, Kirsty, it's never hurt for years. It just gets a bit stiff, that's all.'

Nevertheless, she'd be loath to leave him unattended in the house, even though he'd promised to sleep most of the time and he'd taken a sedative.

'Go on, Kirsty,' he'd urged. 'You don't look at all well yourself. You're needing a change. It'll do you the world of good to get out.'

And indeed, the ride in Greg's car and the visit to his cheerful flat did help to take her mind off things, and to make her feel much better.

'Glad you came?' he asked in the car on the way back to Botanic Crescent later that night.

'Mm.' Snuggling close to him, she felt almost happy. She strained her face round so that she could see her mother in the back seat, propped up with cushions and swathed in a tartan travelling rug. 'You enjoyed yourself too, didn't you, Mum?'

'Yes, indeed I did, dear.'

'Here we are.' Greg drew the car up at the front door of the house. 'Back again. I'll help Mum out, Kirsty, if you open the door.'

It was then, with the thought of stepping back into the house, that all the fear, all the strain, returned. She didn't want to go in. And she certainly didn't want Greg to go in with her. She stood holding the key in the lock, too terrified to move a muscle.

'Wake up, darling,' Greg called out good-humouredly. 'You mustn't sleep yet. It's too cold out here.'

She turned the key and pushed the door open.

'I'll go through to the kitchen and put the kettle on,' she called out in a loud voice, as much for Johnny's benefit as Greg's. 'You take Mum into the sitting room.'

She was just passing the sitting room as she uttered the words. Then suddenly she halted in her tracks. The door lay wide to the wall and the mess it revealed was incredible. The place had been ruthlessly ransacked. Chairs were upturned, and cushions and ornaments strewn all around. Books had been flung onto the floor, the carpet torn up, and furniture hauled around.

Just in time, Kirsty jerked the door shut.

'No, on second thoughts, Mum,' she turned to her mother and Greg who was helping her into the house, 'you'd better go straight to bed and I'll give you your hot drink there. The sitting-room fire's out and it's bitterly cold. I'll switch on the electric fire in your bedroom. You'll be nice and cosy there.'

'Yes, all right, dear. It's long past my bedtime. And I must admit, I am a little tired.'

Her mother safely installed in the bedroom, Kirsty pulled the bedroom door shut and beckoned to Greg. 'Just look in the sitting room,' she whispered. 'Thank goodness Mum didn't see it.'

'Whew!' Greg whistled as his grey eyes took stock of the

upheaval. 'You've had a visitor. And by the looks of things, he's given this room such a thorough going-over that he hasn't had time to do anywhere else. At least your mother's room wasn't touched. But I'd better check the other rooms. Hey! He could still be hiding somewhere in the house.'

Before Kirsty could stop him, he suddenly raced upstairs, his long muscular legs taking two and three steps at a time.

'Greg . . .' In sudden panic she flew after him.

'Greg . . .'

# 28

The plate of salmon Betty had left out for her mother had gone. At least that was a relief. Her mother was not going to starve. Though why should she care? Because, she supposed, she was not as bad as she thought she was, and certainly not as bad as her mother thought she was. The television was still on. That meant, as she suspected, that her mother had acquired a taste for it while watching it in the hospital. That was a relief as well. As long as she left enough food in the house and the television on, she didn't need to feel guilty about leaving her mother while she was at the Art School or out with her friends. And one day her mother would probably make a full recovery. By that time, hopefully, Betty would be able to cope with the tirade of vicious words of hate her mother would bombard her with.

Meantime, it was part of her own recovery to be honest with the others in her group at the Art School. She had even told them that she wrote poetry. They were intrigued.

Tommy said, 'Of course, it's another branch of creativity. And if you are truly creative in one area, you will be creative in others.'

'Bring your poems in and read them to us,' the others pleaded.

Betty blushed. 'Oh no, I couldn't do that.'

'Why not? They can't be that bad.'

'It's not that.'

'What then?'

'It's . . . It's because they're a bit sexy.'

'Ooh! Now you definitely must let us hear them.'

Betty managed a weak laugh. 'Well, actually, they're very sexy.'

'Bring them in tomorrow, do you hear?'

'Well, all right,' Betty agreed reluctantly. 'But I'll give you a copy each to read to yourselves. I couldn't possibly read them out loud or listen to them being read out loud. I'd die of embarrassment.'

They were all alight with excitement and glee and assured her that they could hardly wait until the next day. Meanwhile, Betty took some of her poems to PDC Copyprint in Douglas Street and had copies made so that she could give one to each of her friends. That night she couldn't sleep for hours, wondering what on earth they'd think of her once they'd read the poems.

Even when she did sleep, her mind was whirling with feverish words: 'His hands. His skin stroking the skin on my arms, providing a harmony of heat. Not a moment too soon, his hand moves to other parts of me, not stopping until the final sharp, hot gasp.'

The next morning she left some breakfast for her mother in the kitchen and something in the fridge for lunch. A large tin of mixed biscuits that she'd bought the day before also lay ready for use if necessary. It contained some rich tea and digestives, her mother's favourites.

Betty told her mother, 'I don't know when I'll be back. We're very busy at the Art School just now. We're working hard to have enough ready for the show. I need to try very hard to get a degree. That way I could get a regular job as a teacher and be financially independent.'

Her mother just glared back at her. No change there then, Betty thought. No matter what she did, her mother would go on hating her until the day she died.

As soon as she arrived at the Art School, all her friends pounced on her and demanded a copy of the poems. Blushing again, she obliged. Very soon, there were cries of, 'They're really good, Betty. Really, really good.'

Hamish Ferguson said, 'Good? They're bloody wonderful. Talk about hiding your light under a bushel! Fancy you being able to write poetry like that. You've real talent, Betty.'

Her embarrassment was overwhelmed by delight. 'You honestly think so?'

'Of course,' everyone agreed.

'I enjoy writing poetry. I always find it such a happy release. Especially when I was so dominated and made so miserable by my mother. But I never thought it was any good.'

'Well, it is,' Hamish assured her. 'It's good enough to be published.'

Betty could have hugged him. She had never paid any attention to him, or to any of the male students, before. The only man she ever had eyes for was Greg McFarlane. Now she saw a young man with short brown spiky hair and brown eyes. He was a bit on the plump side and he had a few pimples but they were set in a kind face. She remembered how he had been badly beaten up and she had been so caught up in her own problems at the time that she'd never even given him a word of sympathy. She felt guilty about that now.

'Thanks, Hamish, but I'd have to write a lot more of them before I'd have enough to be published. Maybe I will after we get all the work done for the show. That has to take priority now, hasn't it?'

She began setting up her easel and the others followed suit. This time, Betty looked over at Hamish's easel. He had put it up next to hers.

'You've plenty of talent yourself, Hamish.'

'You think so?'

'Definitely.'

He looked pleased as he turned his attention back to the canvas. They worked in concentrated silence after that until break time. Then, as they all crowded over to the rec with students from all the other departments, Hamish chatted to Betty about what he wanted to do after the course finished and the show was over.

'I'd like to travel overseas for a few months before I settle down. Get a bit more experience of the world.'

'Gosh, that sounds great. I've never been out of Glasgow.'

'Never been out of Glasgow?' Hamish echoed incredulously. 'Not even to Edinburgh or Oban or the Highlands and Islands?'

'No, honestly. My mother always had this awful routine and never went further than Sauchiehall Street. But she even stopped going there because it had become so common, she said. All the high-class, respectable shops she used to know had gone.'

'Gosh, I've had just the opposite experience. My mother was always moving me around. But your experience is soul-destroying, Betty. You've got to start getting out and around.' He hesitated, then blurted out, 'How about us going through to Edinburgh on Saturday? Spend the day there. I could show you around.'

Betty could have danced with joy. 'Oh Hamish, that would be great. I'd love to see Edinburgh.'

Hamish shook his head in disbelief. 'I can hardly credit that you've never even seen our capital city. It's so beautiful and fascinating, Betty. There's so much there to see.'

'Oh thanks, Hamish. I'll really look forward to Saturday now.'

She had been dreading it before. The thought of not having

to go to the School and instead being shut up with her mother all day had been the stuff of nightmares. Now she could hardly wait for Saturday to come.

They met at Queen Street Station quite early in the morning. Betty was a bit nervous, but Hamish gently took charge. He'd already got return tickets, so he ushered her to the platform. They boarded the train and searched through the carriage to get a seat with a table all to themselves. Shyly they squashed in side by side. Betty chattered at first, but gradually relaxed as Hamish pointed out the various views and detailed his plans for the coming day. They shared a bar of fruit and nut chocolate and she happily realised that there was a definite rapport between them. To her surprise, they really got on and there were no awkward silences.

The train slowed as it drew through the outskirts of the city. Breathlessly, Betty craned her neck to see the huge bulk of the castle rock looming on the right as the train slowly pulled into the station.

'The New Town has lots of interest as well, but for your first trip, I think we need to have a wee stroll up to the Castle.'

They ambled up the steep curving street crammed with interesting boutiques, pubs and little shops that catered to a wide variety of cult groups. Goths and punks, students and tourists mingled as they wandered along. When they reached the Royal Mile, they turned right up towards the Castle, the shops here awash with tartan. Buskers playing everything from pipes to didgeridoos were on every corner, vying for the attention of the thronging crowd. Occasionally, little passages could be seen leading off between the ancient buildings, leading to all sorts of mysteries.

As they approached the esplanade in front of the Castle, the whole panorama of Edinburgh lay before them. The view was spectacular, and the strong wind that tugged at clothes and hair gave added depth to the dramatic views.

Hamish told her that William Wordsworth had said when he'd gazed out at the city's dramatic outline, 'Stately Edinburgh, throned on crags.'

The castle dominated the skyline from all sides. It towered high above everything else.

'You should see it at night,' Hamish said. 'When it's floodlit.'

'Oh, I can just imagine. It must look wonderful.'

'We'll come some time at night and see it if you like.'

'Oh yes.'

'Right, let's go up to the Castle just now and look down at the view of Edinburgh. Especially the Royal Mile. It leads down from the Castle to Holyrood Palace and of course the Scottish Parliament.'

More than that, on the way up, they came to what Hamish said was an outlook tower, and a small pipe protruding from its white domed roof was in fact a periscope.

'It's called Camera Obscura. You can see a wonderful bird's-eye view of the city projected through a series of lenses and mirrors.'

After walking around inside the Castle and seeing the Scottish crown jewels, they walked down again to the Royal Mile. They went into the Writers' Museum in Lady Stair's Close, where the works of Robert Louis Stevenson, Robert Burns, Sir Walter Scott and Robert Fergusson lived on.

Stevenson wrote of Edinburgh, 'The delicate did die early, and I, as a survivor, among bleak winds and plumping rain, have been sometimes tempted to envy them their fate.'

Across the road in Riddle's Court was where the eighteenth-century philosopher David Hume once lived. Then there was Brodie's Close, the house of William Brodie, the real-life basis for Robert Louis Stevenson's story of Dr Jekyll and Mr Hyde.

Hamish decided it was time to go for something to eat.

'Come on, I know a wee French restaurant down by the Grassmarket that's not too expensive, but really good.'

The restaurant was really small, with natural stone walls and old, distressed wooden flooring. All the furniture was stained a faded pale blue. Tea lights and candles were scattered randomly around the two small rooms. Betty was entranced at the decor and the ambience.

Hamish suggested the set two-course meal, and it looked lovely. Betty realised of course that part of the attraction for Hamish would be the discounted cost, so she quickly agreed that it did seem to be the tastiest option. They were both delighted with the duck and cranberry pâté served with thick flaky home-made oatcakes and a side salad. For the main course, they had medallions of venison with a rich, fruity sauce, and fennel and garlic potatoes, all washed down with a glass of house red.

'Are you enjoying it all?' Hamish asked when they eventually left the restaurant.

Betty linked her arm through his and hugged it tight. 'Oh yes, thank you for bringing me, Hamish.'

He had never felt so happy before in his life. He patted the hand that was clinging to his arm. 'I'm so glad.'

Betty's heart was full of gladness too.

# 29

Her eyes stretched wide with anxiety, Kirsty listened to Greg purposefully striding in and out of all the bedrooms. She reached the top of the stairs in a matter of seconds, but so out of breath that she found herself unable to utter a word.

He didn't see her at first, standing speechless and white-faced on the landing. He had come to a halt in the doorway of Johnny's room, his whole attention riveted on the scene inside.

Kirsty's heart thumped loudly and painfully. What was Greg staring at? Surely Johnny wouldn't have been so foolish as to come down to his room for anything? She'd warned him not to and he'd promised. But no, it couldn't be Johnny. He'd be sound asleep. Hadn't she given him one of her mother's sedatives for this very reason?

'Greg,' she managed at last, 'for pity's sake, don't just stand there. Tell me what's wrong.'

Thoughtfully, he looked around at her. 'That's odd.'

'What do you mean?'

'Look in here.'

Kirsty approached the bedroom door. Just like the sitting room downstairs, Johnny's room had been completely turned upside down and ransacked.

'Why should a burglar . . .' Greg murmured to himself,

'. . . walk past these two rooms on the landing, then that first one along the corridor and choose instead the one at the end?'

Kirsty cleared her throat. 'Oh, I shouldn't think it was a matter of choice, Greg. He just happened to go into that room, that's all.'

'What?' Greg scoffed. 'He "just happened" to go into the furthest away and most inaccessible room in the house? No, it looks to me as if this crook was searching for something . . . Something he imagined he would most likely find in one of two rooms – the sitting room or Johnny's room.' He hesitated. 'But what? What could it be? That's the odd thing. Have you any idea?'

Kirsty shook her head, anger for the moment snatching away fear. The identity of the burglar had suddenly occurred to her. Who else would it be but Paul Henley searching for the money? Her nails dug into her palms. Of course, Paul would know that she couldn't do anything about this despicable afternoon's work.

He'd wasted his time, though. For he hadn't found the money.

As she followed Greg back downstairs, her mind groped towards the whole truth. It was as she'd suspected from the start. Paul didn't care about Johnny. He had no intention of getting him out of the country. All Paul wanted was the money.

Her brow puckered. And yet, as Johnny said, Paul couldn't just leave him here. The safety and success of the whole plan depended on everyone believing Johnny was dead and that the manager was the one who'd run off with the contents of the safe.

Then gradually everything fitted into place and made sense. Paul had boasted from the start that he'd thought of the perfect plan to get away with the robbery and murder. All Paul needed to do was to murder Johnny. Only one thing was keeping

Johnny alive – knowledge of where the money was hidden. If Paul found it, Johnny wouldn't stand a chance. Here indeed was the perfect crime. Johnny Price was already dead and buried.

'Kirsty, you look as white as a sheet. Not that I'm surprised,' Greg said grimly. 'You've had more than enough to face recently without this.'

'What are you doing?' Dazedly she watched him snatch up the telephone and begin punching out numbers.

'Phoning the police, of course.'

'No, you can't. You mustn't.' She rushed towards him. 'Greg, please. Think of Mother. She can't have crowds of policemen milling all over the house. She's tired. You heard her say so yourself. Oh please, Greg.'

He cupped the receiver against his ear but clamped a broad palm over the mouthpiece. 'Calm down.' His voice was gentle, yet she detected a very firm undercurrent to it. 'There isn't going to be a crowd. A detective and perhaps a fingerprint man, two or three at the most. I'll speak to Jack.'

'But Mother will hear them,' she cried desperately, 'and she'll find out about the burglary.'

'Nonsense. She's still taking a nightly sedative. I saw you give it to her with her hot drink. Anyway, we can all give you a hand to clear up the mess. You'd never manage to get the place back to normal on your own before morning.'

'Yes, I will. I will. Quite easily. Greg, put down the phone. Please, just forget about all of this.'

'You're being ridiculous, Kirsty.'

Turning abruptly away from him, she made her way blindly to the kitchen. Her hands shakily sought one of the kitchen chairs and, sinking into it, she closed her eyes. She didn't think she could stand the strain of several detectives in the house. They weren't going to be just 'in the house', that was the trouble. They'd be searching, prodding, peering around. Three or more pairs of eyes would be ferreting about and finding everything.

'Darling, try not to worry.' Greg came into the kitchen and quietly closed the door. 'I've told them to come round the back way so as not to ring the front doorbell. Everything's going to be all right.'

She just stared at him, her brown eyes dark with tragedy.

'Honey, don't look at me like that.' He came over beside her and cupped her face in his hands. 'Everything's going to be all right, I tell you. Just relax.'

Still she stared, tense and silent.

'I'm going to make you a good strong cup of tea with plenty of sugar in it. You'll feel better after that. And I'll speak to the police and explain. They'll be in and away in no time. You'll see.'

It was a case of waiting, she thought, waiting in anguished suspense.

Eventually the police arrived. She heard sympathetic voices. She sat staring into the steaming cup of tea that Greg had given her, just waiting.

The words 'poor kid' and 'her mother's illness' and 'her brother's death' and 'now the shock of this' were whispered. She listened, longing to scream at them to hurry up and get on with what they'd come to do. How could they be so cruel? Why must they torment her by even a moment's unnecessary suspense?

'I think I should phone for the doctor,' Greg said. 'I've never seen you like this before.'

'No, Greg.' Summoning what energy she had left, she added, 'The hot drink's made me feel better. All I need now is to get to bed.'

'Of course, darling. There's just one thing we'll need you to do first, providing you feel up to it.'

'Yes, what's that?'

'Have a look around to see what's missing.'

'I've already looked. Nothing's been taken.'

'Are you sure, Kirsty? You haven't had time to look very thoroughly.'

'I'll go round everything again. But there's very little of any value in the house except a few little pieces of jewellery belonging to Mum and that's all right. I checked it while I was in her room.' Kirsty felt the slim gold watch on her wrist and stretched her hand, making the diamond engagement ring on her finger sparkle with reflected light. 'And I'm wearing the only decent jewellery I possess. As for money, I had seven pounds in the desk drawer. The drawer's been pulled out but the money's still there. I saw it the first time I looked in the sitting room.'

'How about letters, private papers? Make a more thorough examination of the desk, Kirsty. And look a lot closer at the room upstairs.' Greg's big hand firmed over her elbow as he helped her to her feet. 'It really looks as if this has something to do with Johnny.'

'Something . . . Something to do with Johnny?' She faltered.

'Yes. Did Johnny ever keep anything of value in his room?'

She shook her head.

'Try to remember, Kirsty. Think about it and look at his room very carefully. Then afterwards, straight to bed. I'll tidy both rooms. Then I'll bunk down in Johnny's bed for the night.'

'But Greg . . .' Her eyes widened with apprehension. 'You can't.'

'Of course I can. I'm not going to leave you and Mum alone in the house after all this. No, I'm staying right here for the rest of the weekend. Until your father gets back, if necessary.'

'But your work . . .'

'I can go on my shift if necessary, but I'm staying here

overnight.' He squeezed her arm affectionately. 'So stop worrying. That's an order.'

Kirsty tried to smile but her mind was still in turmoil. She hardly knew what she was doing or saying for the next twenty minutes or so. Even after she'd gone to bed, the problem of Greg being in the house for the next few days or nights swamped her brain and completely exhausted her. For hours she lay wide-eyed clutching the bedclothes up to her chin, thinking about the utter impossibility of the situation. A terrible suspicion was beginning to nag at her. Apart from anything else, the strain of trying to act her normal self to Greg might prove too much.

Once or twice recently, she'd noticed him staring thoughtfully at her and his unblinking scrutiny had proved most unnerving. There were times when she'd felt herself teetering nearer and nearer to hysteria and yet it was imperative that she mustn't break down. Especially in front of Greg, she couldn't afford to show unusual emotion.

If she could just keep calm and hang on for a few more days. She needed time to speak to Paul. He had to be forced to get a ship for Johnny quickly. She had to make Paul see he hadn't a chance of getting a penny unless he kept his promise to Johnny first.

Would it be too dangerous to phone the club where he worked, she wondered? She had to get in touch with him tomorrow somehow. He had to be warned about Greg being in the house and told when it would be safe to come and discuss the final arrangements.

She dreaded the idea of meeting Paul again. She remembered how he'd looked at her and the way he'd held her. Sleep came eventually but it was only a restless, nightmarish interlude before morning, when she woke and immediately scrambled up in bed.

The detectives couldn't have found Johnny or they would

have told her hours ago. He must still be hiding. He still had a chance. But Greg would be in Johnny's room now, lying in Johnny's bed. Immediately above him in the loft, Johnny might be up and limping about. Greg would hear him. Somehow she must warn Johnny and explain to him what had happened. He'd be in an awful state already. The paraffin heater would be empty again and his food and drink would be finished.

She dressed hurriedly. The sooner she got breakfast under way and Greg out of Johnny's room, the better. But how could she get food to Johnny? That was the problem.

She thought of nothing else all day, although at the same time talking and acting quite normally with Greg and her mother. At least, she tried very hard to behave coolly and calmly, until her mother suddenly announced, 'Kirsty, I've made up my mind. I'm going to accept Aunt Jess's invitation to stay with her for a wee holiday. And you're going to go over to Kirklee Terrace and stay with Greg. I phoned Simon and he's all for it. Simon says the change will do me good and his sister is such a cheery soul. She'll be good company for me. And he's quite right.'

'Great,' Greg agreed.

Kirsty shook her head, at the same time frantically searching for a believable excuse to stay in the house.

'I'd love to, of course, darling,' she murmured, averting her face from his, 'but not right now. I honestly don't think I'd be able to muster enough energy.'

'Greg could take you in the car, dear,' Mrs Price insisted. 'And after all, it's only a few minutes away from here but so much cheerier, dear. This house is so sad just now. I can feel the sadness in the very air of the place. I'm definitely going to have my wee holiday.'

'Fine, fine. But I'll just stay here,' Kirsty said with a voice that was quiet and restrained, yet vibrated with such strange intensity that Mrs Price and Greg exchanged puzzled looks.

They didn't say any more, but Kirsty knew that they were going to discuss it and her unexpected refusal as soon as her back was turned. It couldn't be helped, though.

Her immediate and most pressing problem was how to organise help for Johnny. Late that night, after Greg was sleeping, would be the only possible time to get help to Johnny, she decided eventually. In the quiet of the night, she could surely get up to the loft without being seen.

Daytime ticked slowly past. She kept glancing again and again at the clock, willing it to go faster. In a fever of impatience, she kept thinking, 'Johnny's upstairs cold and hungry. For nearly two days and a night, he's had little or no warmth and nothing to eat.'

Night came at last and she waited in her bedroom until her watch told her it was after midnight. Surely Greg would be sleeping and it would be perfectly safe now.

She turned the handle of her bedroom door very slowly.

The landing was dark and quiet. She switched on her torch and shone it up at the opening of the loft. She wondered if she ought to go up and see Johnny right away. No, better get all the things collected together that she needed first.

She hurried downstairs on tiptoe, and with the help of her torch she made her way to the kitchen. While the kettle was boiling for the flasks of tea and coffee, she made sandwiches and put them in a tin, then she took the sandwich tin, a can of paraffin and a few other odds and ends upstairs and laid them on the landing floor in readiness for her climb to the loft. The water had boiled by the time she returned to the kitchen and she hastily filled the flasks and switched off the light before tiptoeing back upstairs again.

Quite an odd assortment of articles was now spread out on the landing floor and Kirsty had some difficulty in keeping her feet clear of them in the dark as she struggled to pull down the loft ladder. At last she managed it and she was standing with one foot on the first rung, on her way to push open the loft hatch, when she heard a door creak open. She clicked off her torch, the hatch disappeared, and the darkness was utter and complete. Afraid to move, she remained with her foot on the ladder, her fingers digging into the big metal torch in her hand.

Footsteps were coming cautiously along the corridor. Kirsty shrank back against the wall.

At any moment, someone was going to come around the corner on the landing and literally fall over all the stuff she'd spread out on the landing floor.

Her thoughts jumbled together in wild confusion. Had Paul returned to continue his search? Had he sneaked round the back of the house and climbed a drainpipe into one of the empty bedrooms? Was he now on his way to discover the money in her room?

Or could it be Greg? Had he heard something? Was he coming to investigate?

Suddenly a shadowy figure loomed from the corridor and scattered her thoughts in terror. Like a wild thing, she immediately sprang into action.

The big metal torch cracked down on the figure's head with all the strength she had in her.

Then everything was still and silent again.

A moment or two passed before Kirsty could bring herself to press the switch on the torch and shine the bright beam downwards.

'Greg!' Her cry of horror shattered the quiet of the house. 'Oh Greg, darling, what have I done?'

Greg lay in a crumpled heap at her feat. A splash of bright red blood oozed from the side of his face.

He didn't seem to be breathing.

# 30

The harsh beam of light darted about, slashing at the blackness of the house.

'Greg,' Kirsty repeated.

Above her head, the loft hatch creaked cautiously open and, aiming the light upwards, Kirsty caught her brother's thin, white face. He shrank back, blinking.

'Johnny,' she called to him. 'Johnny, look what I've done.'

Slowly his head reappeared.

'Wait a minute.' She hurried across the landing and switched on the light. 'Johnny, look at him. I'll never be able to forgive myself.'

'Maybe it's not as bad as you think,' Johnny whispered, kneeling down at the other side of Greg's motionless figure and cradling his head in his arm.

Kirsty whispered, 'Hold him until I get a sponge from the bathroom.'

When she returned she bathed the blood from Greg's head.

'It's just a small cut. I can see it now.'

As she spoke, Greg stirred and groaned, making Kirsty and Johnny stare, paralysed, at each other. At any moment, Greg was going to open his eyes and see Johnny crouching over him.

'Get back.' Kirsty was the first to gather her wits together.

'Quick! Carry as much as you can up with you. I'll bring the rest.'

Rushing across the landing, she switched off the light.

'Kirsty, I can't see my way.'

'Sh-sh.' The torch clicked on and flickered impatiently around the ladder. 'For pity's sake, just get up there.'

Like magic the articles which had been strewn all over the landing floor disappeared, Johnny clambered wildly into the loft, and the wooden hatch crashed shut.

In the dark, Kirsty could hear Greg grope shakily to his feet.

'Greg, darling, it's me.' She clicked on the torch to reveal him standing clutching his head, still looking dazed.

'Greg, I'm so sorry. I thought you were the burglar. I couldn't sleep and I was just coming out of my room to go along to the bathroom for some aspirin when I heard footsteps. I panicked and grabbed this torch and the next thing I knew, you were lying unconscious at my feet.'

Greg managed a chuckle of amusement.

'That's a good one. And here was I thinking you needed my protection this weekend.' He laughed again and rubbed his injured head.

'Judging by the wallop you pack, honey, you don't need a bodyguard. You do all right on your own.'

'I'll switch on the light,' Kirsty told him, 'then I'll fetch some sticking plaster for that cut.'

In the bathroom, she swallowed a couple of tablets to steady her nerves. Goodness knows how she'd be able to sleep after all this excitement, she thought. But eventually she did sink thankfully into bed, complete exhaustion overcame her, and she remembered nothing more until morning.

Then before she made breakfast and before Greg came downstairs, she furtively dialled the number of the casino where Paul and Renee worked. With the receiver clutched against her cheek, she kept an eye on the sitting-room door in case Greg appeared.

The dialling tone burr-burred with infuriating monotony.

'Oh hurry, hurry,' she whispered in exasperation. 'What's keeping you? What's wrong?'

Then she realised that the casino would not be open yet. There would be no one there to answer the phone. Hastily she scribbled a note to Paul instead, warning him that Greg was staying at the house but that she'd persuade him to leave by Tuesday lunch-time:

'. . . Could you come and see me about four o'clock? It'll be safe by then. Greg will be at work and my mother will be in bed. She's been taking a rest every afternoon . . .'

Then, struggling into her coat, she stuffed the note into an envelope and slipped stealthily out of the house to post it.

When Tuesday came, she told Greg, 'Of course you must go back home and go to work tonight, Greg. There's no reason why you shouldn't. I'm perfectly all right now. I'll be back at work tomorrow morning.'

A smile hovered on Greg's mouth but his eyes surveyed her thoughtfully. 'You seem in an awful hurry to get rid of me.'

'Don't be daft. We'll see each other tomorrow at the station. I'm just worrying about you taking so much time off work on my account. There's no need, really.'

'Mm . . . Well, I'll leave at lunch-time but I'll have to go home first for a change of clothes, etcetera. There's a couple of things I need to collect too.'

'I'll tell you what.' Kirsty smiled. 'We could go for a walk or something.'

'Good idea,' Greg agreed. 'It's cold but you can wrap up well and we'll step out and soon have the roses back in those cheeks of yours. How about you, Mum?' He turned to Mrs Price, chuckling. 'Come on, where's your hiking boots? Jump to it.'

Mrs Price laughed and shook her head. 'You're an awful lad. Away you go with Kirsty. It's time she had a breath of fresh air. Apart from that run in your car to your place, she hasn't been out for days.'

Arm in arm with Greg, the strength of him close to her and the crisp wind whisking at her hair, Kirsty felt happier and more confident than she'd done since the whole terrible business with Johnny started. She would manage to cope after all. She'd make sure that Johnny was looked after. No one, not even Paul Henley, would be allowed to lay a finger on her brother.

'Kirsty, look up there.' Greg's deep authoritative voice suddenly scattered her thoughts.

They had been down to Kelvingrove Park and the surrounding area and were now returning from another direction. They were approaching the back of the house and it was at the house that Greg was pointing.

'What?' she murmured cautiously. 'I don't see anything.'

'The loft.'

'The loft?' Her heart raced with panic. 'What about the loft?'

'The skylight's open.'

'Shouldn't it be?'

'I've never noticed it open before. Hey, I wonder if . . .'

'Oh stop it, Greg.' She managed a laughing, teasing voice. 'For goodness' sake, what a suspicious man you are. You really should have been a policeman. I was up in the loft the other day putting some more stuff out of the way. I opened the window, silly. It was so dusty and airless, I could hardly breathe.'

She could hardly breathe now, so terrified was she that Greg might pursue the subject further. But her luck held and, apparently quite satisfied with her explanation, he said no more about it.

Nor did he show any uneasiness about her suggestion that he should leave Botanic Crescent. She couldn't really relax, however, until she actually said goodbye to him.

She peered at her watch, willing Paul to hurry.

Johnny's life could depend on how she handled Paul this afternoon. She must threaten to destroy the money – surely that would force him to keep his promise and get Johnny safely on board a ship within the next day or two.

When at last she saw his car approaching, she hurried to open the front door before the bell rang.

'Thank goodness! I thought you were never coming.'

'No need to worry, beautiful. I'd never miss an opportunity of visiting you.'

'Nor would I, darling.' The sarcastic voice from behind Paul startled Kirsty.

'Oh, it's you, Renee.' Although she had no liking for the woman, she hadn't been looking forward to being alone with Paul and so she felt quite glad to see her.

Once they were in the sitting room, Kirsty said, 'I'll come to the point as quickly as possible. I sent that note because I especially wanted to see you today. I wanted to tell you that I know where the money is. And I'm going to destroy it, burn every paper note in the bag.'

'You wouldn't dare,' Renee said.

'Oh, wouldn't I? Wouldn't I just . . .'

Paul stared at her. 'You know, Renee, I believe she would.'

'Another thing I want to make clear,' Kirsty went on. 'You'd better not try laying a finger on Johnny. And no more lies or wasting time. I'm warning you, if you don't get him safely on board a ship before next week, you'll never see a penny of that money.'

'Why, you little . . .' Renee took a step forward, but immediately Paul gripped her arm.

'Take it easy. Everything's going to work out exactly as we

planned.' Then he turned to Kirsty. 'There's no need to get nasty. We're friends of Johnny's, remember. I'll get him out of the country all right.'

'But it must be within the next week,' Kirsty insisted. 'That's the whole point of sending for you today. To impress on you how impossible it is for Johnny to stay here more than another few days. For one thing, his health's in danger. And for another, any day now, my boyfriend's going to start asking questions. Not only that, my father is due back soon from down south. And don't forget you and Renee are in this too. It's not just Johnny who'll suffer.'

Suddenly her attention switched away from them. 'What was that?'

Then suddenly and unmistakably, the doorbell rang, bringing both Paul and Renee running.

'What do you bet, that's your bloody firefighter now,' Paul hissed.

'No, he didn't say he was coming back.'

Kirsty walked across the hall.

'Greg darling,' she faltered in surprise when she opened the front door, 'I didn't expect to see you again today.'

He walked past her into the house. 'I decided to check that you and Mum were all right before I go on duty.'

'Mum slept late. I was just going to waken her after my visitors left. Paul and Renee . . . They're just going.' She gave a little laugh. 'I'm certainly being well looked after today. Paul and Renee called to see if we were all right too.'

'Oh?' Greg's keen grey eyes studied the two of them. 'That's interesting.'

'Well, we'll be seeing you, Kirsty.' Paul propelled Renee towards the door.

'Yes, and thanks for calling.'

Kirsty struggled to appear normal and pleasant to both of them when ushering them out.

'See you again soon,' she called, and waved as their car slid away.

'What was that all about?' Greg demanded when she came back into the sitting room.

'What do you mean?' Guiltily she avoided his stare.

'Come on, Kirsty. I'm no fool. That gruesome twosome didn't come here out of the kindness of their hearts, or concern for you and Mum.'

'Well, that's what they told me. And after all, they were friends of Johnny's, Greg. I couldn't very well turn them away.'

Greg's eyes narrowed thoughtfully. 'What's his name again?'

'Paul Henley.'

'What does he do? Where does he work?'

She hesitated, then said unhappily, 'Darling, does it matter? Why do you want to know about him?'

'He interests me.'

'Are you staying for tea?' she asked, in an effort to change the subject. 'I'm just going through to the kitchen to put the kettle on.'

'No, I'd better be off again, Kirsty. Sure you're OK?'

'Yes.' She smiled. 'Fine.'

'See you tomorrow at the station, then.'

As soon as she closed the door on his retreating figure, uneasiness descended on her. She went through to the kitchen to prepare the tea, all the time wondering what was going on in Greg's mind.

She lit the gas under the kettle and it hissed loudly through the quietness. The only other sound was the gentle tinkling of the cat's bell as it came into the kitchen and went over to its saucer of milk.

Then, suddenly, there were other sounds. A thumping, a noise of running feet, the kitchen door crashing open.

'Johnny!' she gasped. 'Have you gone mad? Why are you down here? What's wrong?'

He made a pathetic picture, black curls damp and tousled, thin face crimson bright and glistening with fever, blue eyes agitated.

'Kirsty, I couldn't stand it a moment longer. I've caused you enough trouble. God knows what might happen next. I've a terrible feeling that you're in as much danger as me now and I can't stand it, Kirsty. I must do something about it. I must do something before it's too late.'

Before Kirsty had time to stop him, he turned and fled wildly from the kitchen.

'Johnny, come back!' Cutlery clattered onto the floor as she bumped the table aside and rushed after him into the hall. She'd just managed to catch hold of his arm when a door beside them opened unexpectedly. It was their mother's bedroom door.

'Kirsty!' Mrs Price cried out. 'Kirsty, what are you doing?'

# 31

'Where did you get the bump?' one of the firefighters asked. 'Has Kirsty been going for you?'

'As a matter of fact,' Greg laughed, 'it was Kirsty. She mistook me for a burglar in the dark and cracked her torch over my head.'

'What were you both wandering about in the dark for?'

'You might well ask.' Greg turned serious. 'There's something wrong in that house, and I'm determined to find out what it is.'

Just then, Jack Campbell appeared in the doorway.

'Greg, I can't wait. I'm due in the station in a few minutes. But I thought you'd be interested in the result of our enquiries. That guy Paul Henley you asked about has a clean record but here's what's interesting. He works as a croupier in the casino in Buchanan Street. There was a big theft reported there and he was the witness who said he saw the manager leaving carrying a case.' Campbell shrugged. 'According to Henley, the manager usually goes to the bank about that time and he never thought anything about it. But the manager never came back and the safe was found empty.'

'Yes, that is interesting,' Greg said. 'Thanks, Jack.'

After Jack Campbell had hurried away, Greg repeated, 'Very interesting.'

'You think this Henley guy is in on the robbery or something?' one of the others asked.

'Could be. I don't know. But for some reason, he's been hanging about Botanic Crescent. He's up to something. I've been suspicious about him from the moment I set eyes on him. I think I'd better phone Simon.'

'Kirsty's father?'

'Yes. He didn't want to go away and leave Kirsty and her mother alone just now, but Mrs Price insisted that they would be just fine. Then Simon suggested that Mrs Price should go and stay with his sister for a holiday.' He took out his mobile and was just about to dial a number when the alarm bell filled the room with its ear-splitting jangle.

'Bugger!' Greg flung his mobile aside and raced away with all the other firefighters.

On board the engine was a vehicle data system which gave them operational procedures, maps, operational risk assessments, and detailed layouts of all the rooms, as well as information on where water supplies could be found, and on whether there were any chemicals and where they were located.

It was a factory fire. The heat was intense as Greg and his crew approached the fire. The roaring noise of the flames was loud in his ears as they directed the high-pressure jets of water at the base of the flames. Sweat trickled down Greg's face as waves of heat flowed over him. The smell of burning plastic was acrid in his nose. He jerked as something seemed to explode at his feet. He looked round to see a small group of capering teenagers laughing and throwing bottles and stones at the fire crew. They fought to ignore the yobs as they struggled to control the inferno. How easy it would have been to turn the hose on their tormentors. If only!

Luckily, the police arrived a couple of minutes later in squad cars and the yobs moved back. At least now the fire crew could concentrate on the job at hand.

They had to use the longest extending ladder to rescue a man from one of the top windows. Greg was glad of his breathing equipment. Smoke was already belching out of the place and flames were shooting up from the roof. Before Greg could reach him, the man had slid away inside the room, overcome by the smoke. Greg managed to lean inside the window, grab the man with one hand, and haul him back up. Flames had caught on the man's clothing and Greg fought to put them out, and then slung the man over his shoulder. This was anything but easy as the man was very heavily built, but thanks to much practice through the years and many hours in the gym to strengthen his muscles, Greg managed it. He carried the man down to safety and the care of the ambulance crew who were now waiting below. Hoses kept aiming at the flames until at last they got the fire under control, but not before Greg and one of the other firefighters had rescued several terrified people.

They had barely returned to the station when there was another turn out. This time it was to a road accident. They were having to deal with an ever-increasing number of road rescues.

Mostly they involved teenagers or guys in their early twenties who had been drinking or speeding to show off. Or both. He was glad that a scheme had started in schools where they set up a car that had been in a collision and a make-up artist painted injuries on the young people who were supposed to be in the car. The appearance of the very bloody-looking injuries was meant to shock, and it did. Along with this, driving lectures and instruction were given to the schoolchildren, in the hope that they would become good and sensible divers once they were old enough to hold a licence.

The horrific road accidents the firefighters had so often to deal with were such a waste of young lives. 'Young people like you,' they'd tell the schoolchildren, 'who have all your lives before you. All wasted, all gone.' The kids seemed to appreciate these afternoon visits. More and more schools were joining the scheme.

Once back in the station again, Greg thought about what Jack Campbell had told him and he decided to pay the casino a quick visit just to see the lie of the land, apart from anything else. He wasn't quite sure why, but he felt he needed to see the place where the Henleys worked. It turned out that getting into the place was neither quick nor easy. He had to stand at a counter in the entrance area and answer a whole lot of questions about himself, and produce his credit card as a means of identification. A camera behind the counter also took a photograph of him. Eventually, they clicked a door open from behind the counter and he could walk into the main casino area. It was a really luxurious place with many chandeliers hanging from the ceiling. Beneath his feet was a luxuriously thick red and gold fitted carpet. And all around the walls and in the centre of the huge room were gaming machines and tables.

Upstairs there were small tables attractively set with white linen tablecloths and napkins. Greg sat at one of the tables and saw on one side of him an outside balcony that looked down on the river. On the other side of where he sat, he could see down into the hall. Eventually he spotted Paul and Renee Henley.

Paul, like all the other male croupiers, wore black. The women croupiers were all in blue. Across from where the Henleys were working, there was a door and Greg noticed a man in a smart grey suit disappearing through it. Could he be the new manager? He looked like someone in authority going into his office. So this must be where Paul Henley, according to his story, witnessed the original manager absconding with the takings.

A waiter came to the table and asked Greg if he would like to order anything.

'Just a cup of coffee, thanks.'

The waiter bowed and within minutes a steaming cup of coffee was placed in front of Greg. While drinking it, he tried to fathom out why he felt so suspicious of the Henleys, especially Paul. He knew there was something, but he didn't know what.

He phoned Simon Price and tried to convey his unease to him. Simon said he'd make arrangements to return to Glasgow, and Botanic Crescent, as soon as possible.

'They want me to stay on here for another week, but I'll definitely refuse now. Thanks for putting me in the picture, Greg.'

'That's OK. See you soon, then.'

'Yes, definitely. Time I was getting back to my students as well. It's getting nearer to the time of their show. I've a lot to organise with that.'

'OK. See you.'

Greg felt a bit better after the conversation with Simon. Now he could go back to Botanic Crescent and tell Kirsty and Mrs Price that everything would soon be back to normal once Simon returned. Kirsty especially could relax. She would have nothing more to worry about.

# 32

'You'll kill Mother if she sees you,' Kirsty whispered frantically, as she jerked Johnny back against the wall at the side of her mother's bedroom door.

Almost at the same time, Mrs Price appeared in the open doorway and repeated anxiously, 'Kirsty, where are you? What are you doing?'

Kirsty mouthed a desperate plea to Johnny, his back pressed against the wall only a few feet away, 'Get back upstairs – for Mum's sake.'

Then she quickly stepped out in front of Mrs Price, blocking her path.

'Mum, I feel a little dizzy. I stumbled against the table in the kitchen and gave myself quite a blow. Do you mind if I sit down on the edge of your bed for a minute?'

'Of course not, dear.' Mrs Price put a comforting arm around her. 'Can I get you a drink of water or something?'

'No, no. I'll be all right. It was silly of me, really. Did you hear the noise? I sent all the cutlery flying.'

Was Johnny past the door and up the stairs yet, she wondered. Surely he wouldn't suddenly reappear in the room.

'Kirsty dear, you're trembling.' The older woman's voice

quickened with concern. 'Just you sit there. I'll fetch a cup of tea.'

And before Kirsty could think of another ruse to stop her, Mrs Price had hurried from the room.

Kirsty's hands flew to her ears to blot out the expected screams of shock her mother would give at seeing Johnny. No sound came, however, except the shuffling of slippered feet, then the familiar tinkle of teacups.

In exquisite relief, Kirsty relaxed. Johnny must have come to his senses again and returned quickly to his hiding place. She could hardly wait to make sure, however, and after tea, on the pretext of washing the dishes, she left her mother in the sitting room and crept quietly up to the loft.

'Johnny, thank goodness!' she gasped when she saw him lying on the narrow camp bed. 'I was afraid you might have run out of the house or something.'

He turned his head towards her. 'I'm beginning to wonder if I'll ever be able to leave this house.'

'Oh Johnny, don't talk like that. You mustn't give up hope. I won't let you.'

'It's no use, Kirsty.' His blue eyes burned huge in a pinched white face. 'It's not going to work. I know it.'

'Now, now, you don't know anything of the kind. If you can just keep calm and hang on for a few more days, you'll be all right. I've had a talk with Paul and made sure he won't keep you waiting much longer.'

'What do you mean?' Johnny raised himself stiffly. 'What did you say to him?'

'I told him I know where the money is and I threatened to burn the lot if he didn't get you on a ship by the end of this week.'

'He wouldn't like that, Kirsty. He'll be furious at you for telling him what to do.'

'I don't care.'

'But you should.' His hands plucked agitatedly at the blankets. 'I don't want you to get hurt. You mustn't say anything else to Paul. Just keep well away from him.'

'All right, all right, dear.' She hastened to soothe him. 'I'll be careful. I promise.'

She returned downstairs, her face clouded with worry. Johnny was looking really ill.

She couldn't get his thin, ghost-like face out of her mind all evening. Even after she'd gone to bed, she lay wide awake thinking about him, seeing his eyes staring at her, feeling the restless agitation of him.

Paul would have to be quick. There was no telling what Johnny might do.

She drifted eventually into an uneasy sleep. A sleep filled with mixed-up dreams and vague apprehension.

She was glad when morning came, yet reluctant to face the day before her. She dressed slowly, then sat at the dressing table absently brushing her hair. No sound of any movement came from the loft above. She listened intently. The house had never been so silent.

Putting down the brush, she tiptoed to the bedroom door and opened it a little. No sound of her mother either. She slipped out of the room. If she was very quiet and careful, perhaps she'd be able to make breakfast for Johnny and take it up to him before her mother woke up.

She'd just reached the stairs when suddenly she felt someone touch her. Already strained to breaking point with worry and lack of proper sleep, she found herself unable to stifle the scream of fright that leapt from her throat.

'Kirsty, Kirsty, don't. It's me. I couldn't stay cooped up in there any longer. I had to start moving around. I've been all over the place all night. I couldn't help it.'

'It's a good job Mum's still on nightly sedation,' Kirsty gasped. 'Goodness knows what she'd have thought if she'd heard me scream like that. It's probably wakened her anyway. And I was hoping to get breakfast safely up to you first.'

'I don't want anything. I'm not hungry.'

'Johnny, you must . . .'

'No, please. I'm too upset to eat.'

'You're not still worrying about me, are you?'

'Yes. I should never have come here. I've never been any good to you. I've caused you nothing but worry and trouble all my life.'

'Nonsense!'

'No, it's the truth.' His mouth trembled. 'I've never realised it till now, when it's only too obvious.'

'Johnny, you're my brother.' She put an affectionate arm around his shoulders. 'I've always been only too glad of the chance to help you. Now, stop being silly. On you go up to the loft and stop worrying. Everything's going to be all right soon, you'll see.'

'I can't go up there again.'

'Yes, you can. Just for another few days.'

She could hear her mother moving about in her room downstairs.

'Johnny,' she repeated, dropping her voice to a whisper, 'you've no choice. You must.'

He nodded, his mouth quivering too much to speak, his eyes moist with an unnatural brilliance. Watching him pull himself up and disappear safely into the loft, Kirsty felt no relief from tension. Her heart – now beating very fast – showed no sign of slowing down.

Johnny couldn't be trusted to stay up there much longer. She didn't blame him, but the tenterhooks of suspense this situation put her on were almost unbearable.

She had to phone Greg and the station to say she needed to take another day off.

'I'm fine but Mum's not so good. I think it would be wrong to leave her here on her own just yet,' she explained.

She hardly knew what she was doing for the rest of the morning.

'Kirsty, what's wrong?'

Startled, she looked up to see Greg striding across the room towards her.

'Greg, what a fright you gave me. I didn't hear you ring the bell.'

'No, I knew Mum would be having her rest. I didn't want to disturb her so I came round through the kitchen. But Kirsty, why are you crying? I've never seen you look so upset.'

Kirsty found a handkerchief and carefully dried her face.

'Oh, I just felt a bit depressed, that's all. I've just left a message on your machine and phoned the station to say I'm OK but I wouldn't be in to work today.'

'That settles it,' he said grimly.

'Settles what?'

'I'm going to get a special licence. We're going to get married immediately.'

The determination that hardened his eyes made her pulse pound with a mixture of excitement and fear. Averting her gaze from his, she said, 'I can't think just now, Greg. Perhaps in a week or two . . .'

'No, right now. I'll see about the licence this afternoon. You won't need to do anything. Don't worry. Leave everything to me.'

'But Greg,' her voice stretched up an octave, 'we can't rush the wedding like this.'

'What's to stop us?'

'My dress isn't ready, for one thing. And Mum can't be left alone just yet. I told you.'

'I can easily move in here until she's a hundred per cent recovered.'

'No, you can't,' Kirsty cried out recklessly. 'I'm sorry, Greg. It's quite impossible.'

His eyes narrowed. 'Why is it impossible?'

'Will you stop interrogating me!' She jumped up, sending her chair crashing back. Colour flamed to her cheeks as her eyes met his.

For a moment or two, he didn't speak. He just stared at her very intently. Then he said in a slow, thoughtful voice, 'It isn't like you to behave like this, Kirsty. Something's going on here, and if it's the last thing I do, I'll get to the bottom of it.'

When the phone rang the next day and she heard Paul Henley's voice, Kirsty closed her eyes in silent thankfulness. But her feelings of relief were short-lived.

'What did you say?' Her voice sharpened with the alertness of incredulity. 'Greg has been to see you, did you say?'

'You heard me! He went to the flat and from there to the casino. He's been asking questions about the robbery.'

'But I never said a word to him about anything.'

'He's got a friend in the force. They've obviously been talking. It's all a matter of time now. We'll have to move fast. That guy's out to get me.'

'But as long as Greg thinks Johnny's dead, there's no way he can find out the truth. There's nothing he can do.'

'I know his type,' Paul rasped bitterly. 'He may be a firefighter but he's acting like a bloody cop. He thinks he's onto something and he'll never let go. I'm telling you, we'll have to move fast. Renee and I will come out to your place tonight. I've got a ship fixed up for Johnny. We'll smuggle him away once it's dark.'

That was settled, then. The uncertainty, the agonising suspense of the past few days was all over. But she still felt apprehensive and afraid.

Paul and Renee mustn't be allowed to get their hands on the money until after Johnny was safely away, she told herself over and over again. It was on the money alone that Johnny's life depended. The thought grew in urgency and she reminded Johnny of it as soon as she managed to get up to the loft. Excitedly, she told Johnny the details of Paul's phone call. Then she said, 'Now, you know our plan, Johnny. I'll come with you and see you safely onto the ship, then I'll drive back here with Paul and Renee and give them the money.'

Nervously Johnny bit his lip. 'I don't feel happy about leaving you alone with them.'

'I'll be perfectly all right. There's no need to worry about me.'

'How can you be so certain?' He stared across at her, agitation twitching at his face and panic filling his eyes. 'Kirsty, something awful could happen.'

'Now, now, you're just working yourself into one of your states, and that won't help either of us. Just you stay here and keep calm until they come for you.'

It wouldn't be long now. Darkness already covered the house like a silent sea of ink. Kirsty eased from the loft and dropped down into the darkness.

Were Paul and Renee already here, she wondered. She'd left the back door unlocked so that they could enter the house soundlessly. She crept downstairs and into the sitting room, and as soon as she switched on the light, she saw the gun.

Paul was lolling back on a chair, the gun in his hand pointing at the door she'd just come through.

'What's the meaning of this?' she asked, suddenly hot with anger, but too conscious of the heavy hush in the house to break it. 'Don't think you'll get anywhere by trying to intimidate me. I'm not so easily frightened.'

Paul too kept his voice low. 'I believe you. I believe you. But your precious brother's not nearly as spunky as you.'

'Just what are you trying to say?'

Paul's face hardened and he jerked to his feet. 'No one

leaves here before I'm in possession of that money. I'm going up to Johnny now and if he doesn't hand it over, I'll beat him with this gun until he's glad to.' He replaced the gun in his pocket and then said, 'You stay here with Renee just now.'

'No, you can't.' Even knowing her mother would be deeply unconscious after the strong sedative she'd given her, Kirsty still kept her voice down as she desperately tried to block the doorway and prevent Paul leaving the room. 'Johnny's weak and ill. He's suffered enough. He panicked and killed a man and I'm not excusing his crime, but these past few days . . .'

'Killed a man?' Paul gave a sarcastic laugh. 'That weakling? He hadn't the guts. Not even in panic.'

Stunned, Kirsty stared at him. 'What do you mean? I don't understand.'

'Your precious brother ran away so fast he didn't notice that the manager was just unconscious. When he'd pushed him away, he'd fallen back and bashed his head, that was all. All I needed to do was bash his head again but a lot harder.'

'Then it was you.' She began to tremble with red-hot fury. 'You killed him. And all this time, you've allowed Johnny, all of us, to suffer. Why you . . . you . . .'

'Don't touch him, Kirsty. Keep back.'

Immediately she swung round.

'Johnny!'

He was standing, grey-faced and huge-eyed, in the doorway.

'You forgot I still have this gun as well as the money, didn't you?' He aimed the weapon at the older man. 'And I'll tell you another thing you didn't know, Paul. I'm perfectly capable of using it to kill you.'

# 33

'No, Johnny, please!' Kirsty hissed. 'You're not a killer. You never murdered anyone. You mustn't let Paul make a murderer of you now. Give that gun to me at once.'

'He got me into all this. Right from the start, it's been all his idea. He deserves to die.'

'Johnny, the law will deal with Paul.'

Johnny had begun to tremble now and two bright blobs of colour glistened on his cheekbones.

'Oh, he's far too clever for the law. Aren't you, Paul? The law's not going to catch you. You've got it all planned. Haven't you?'

'Look, kid . . .' Paul raised his hands. 'Take it easy.'

'Oh, I have been taking it easy, Paul. Cooped up in that loft, I hadn't much choice. I've had plenty of time and opportunity to think, though. I'm not as big a fool as you obviously take me for. I know perfectly well what you were planning to do.'

'All I want is my share of the money, Johnny. It's the money I want, that's all.'

'No, it's not all. You planned to kill both my sister and me. That would have finished everything off very nicely, wouldn't it? With Kirsty and me out of the way, no one could ever have pointed the finger at you.'

He turned a feverish face towards his sister.

'I'm already dead, you see, Kirsty, and another "accident" could easily have been arranged for you. You know too much. He would never have left you here alive. Never have risked you telling Greg.'

'But none of that matters any more,' Kirsty said desperately. 'You're not a murderer. That's all I care about. I'm going to phone and explain the whole thing to Greg.'

'I wouldn't advise it,' Paul said quickly. 'Johnny's still in this up to his neck. He'd be charged with the robbery, for a start, and at least as an accessory to murder.'

'Accessory to murder?' Renee echoed sarcastically. 'He'd be lucky if that was all they flung at him.' She glared venomously at Johnny. 'It's only your word against ours that you didn't kill the manager. I'll swear till I'm blue in the face that Paul was with me all the time from the moment we both left the gaming tables that night.'

Paul moved a step forward. 'So nothing's really changed,' he said.

'Stay where you are!' Johnny brandished the gun at him. 'You're going to die. That's what's different.'

'Wait, Johnny,' Kirsty pleaded. 'You're not giving yourself time to think.'

'No, Kirsty.' He shook his head, at the same time swaying drunkenly. 'It's too late. There's nothing else I can do now.'

'You're ill.' She ran towards him and caught his swaying figure in her arms. 'You need a doctor.'

Suddenly Paul sprang forward. Barging into Kirsty's side and swinging them round against the wall, he wrenched the gun from Johnny's hand.

'All he needs, and all he's going to get, is a bullet in the head.' He pointed the gun, first at Johnny and then at Kirsty, who kept her arms protectively around Johnny's shoulders. 'In fact, if you don't tell me where the money is, right now, both you and your sister will be dead in exactly one minute. Your sister first.'

'No, don't,' Johnny sobbed. 'Please don't hurt Kirsty.'

'The money! The money!'

'It's in her bedroom, in the fireplace, jammed up the chimney.'

'You'd better be telling the truth. Here, Renee, take the gun and watch the pair of them while I go upstairs to check.'

Still clutching Johnny's trembling body close to her, Kirsty watched Paul hurry from the room. Then she waited for a moment or two until she reckoned he'd be across the hall and beginning to ascend the stairs. He'd probably be out of earshot now, she thought. This was an old house and the walls and doors were almost thick enough to be soundproof. She glanced at the table at her side and noted the tall vase of flowers there. To throw the vase at Renee, to take her by surprise and knock the gun from her hand, was their only chance.

She released her hold on Johnny.

'Are you feeling a bit steadier, dear?' she asked gently. But before he could reply, she swooped on the vase and sent it flying across the room.

'Why you . . .' Renee howled in pain as the vase caught her on the side of her head. Then Kirsty was on her, nails hooking and clawing at her face and neck, as she struggled for control of the gun.

They swayed and stumbled across the room, as Kirsty tried to spear Renee's leg or foot with her sharp stilettos.

'Let go! Let go, you bitch,' Kirsty gasped as she frantically wrestled with the older woman. 'Drop it!' Kirsty violently shook and jerked Renee's wrist. 'You'd better do as I say or you're liable to get seriously hurt. I'm a lot stronger than I look. And I'm wearing stiletto heels. If you don't drop that gun, I'll put one right through your foot.'

'Not before I put a bullet through you,' Renee hissed.

'Leave her alone! Get your hands off my sister!'

Out of the corner of her eye, Kirsty saw Johnny come staggering towards her.

As Kirsty's attention was diverted by Johnny's approach, Renee suddenly wrenched herself free and swung the gun up with two hands to face them both.

'Johnny, get back,' she warned. 'Both of you get back. I'm going to enjoy doing this,' she said, 'and I'll be saving Paul some time.'

'You're mad.' Kirsty's voice held a confident tone that she was far from feeling. 'You'll never get away with it.'

'No?' Renee sneered. 'Just watch me.'

The gun was raised. Kirsty faced it coolly, although she was secretly trembling inside. The finger on the trigger tightened.

Unexpectedly, Johnny flung himself forward between Kirsty and the gun, using his body as a shield.

'Johnny!'

The gun hardly made a sound as the bullet sank into Johnny's flesh. He dropped to the floor, bright blood pulsing from his chest as his fingers twitched pathetically at the wound.

Helpless with horror, Kirsty stood staring at her brother now lying still and silent at Renee's feet.

'Leave him alone!' She came to life when Renee bent down and pushed Johnny's inert body roughly aside.

As Johnny had fallen to the floor, he had grabbed at the gun, knocking it from Renee's clutches. She was pulling at him to get at the gun that lay trapped under his inert body.

Kirsty rushed forward in desperation, and her shoulder caught the bent figure of Renee square in her side, knocking her across the room.

Kirsty scrabbled under Johnny's side and swung up the gun, her fingers slippery with Johnny's blood. She immediately levelled it at the other woman. With her free hand, she lifted the receiver off its hook and rapidly dialled 999.

Perspiration pricked her brow and her attention kept straying from Renee to the telephone and then to the sitting-room door. At any moment, Paul was going to return.

The voice at the other end of the phone seemed very far away.

'Tell Sergeant Jack Campbell that Paul and Renee Henley are trying to kill me and my brother.' Trembling violently, she kept the phone clamped to her ear. At last she heard Jack Campbell's voice.

'Is that you, Kirsty?'

'Yes, please come as fast as you can, and tell Greg.'

'A police car will be there in minutes. And I'll phone Greg right now.'

Kirsty replaced the receiver.

'Oh, hurry, hurry,' she thought.

She saw the sitting-room door open but the thunderous drumming of her heart blotted out sound.

'Get over there beside Renee.' She jerked the gun at Paul to emphasise her words. 'And don't try anything. I've already phoned the police. They'll be here at any moment to arrest the pair of you.'

Panic scuttled over Paul's face.

'What happened?' he asked Renee.

'He rushed me and knocked the gun out of my hand, and she grabbed it. You shouldn't have left me with the two of them.'

'I had to check if the money was there.'

'I could have done that, you fool. A lot of good it'll do us now.'

'Oh, I don't know . . .'

The words were barely out of his mouth when he suddenly sent the canvas money bag flying across the room to hit Kirsty a blow on the shoulder. She staggered back with a cry of pain and before she could recover her balance, Paul was across the room and wrenching the gun from her hand.

Immediately, Kirsty wriggled free of him and rushed from the room. She ran across the silent hall and up the stairs. The place was in complete darkness but she knew the house so well, it only took a few moments to reach the loft ladder on the top landing.

Her shoes made a quick clicking sound on the ladder's rungs. Then she hoisted herself up into the loft and shut the hatch.

Without waiting to switch on the light, she pushed and strained at the nearest, heaviest packing case until it sat over the hatch to prevent it from being opened again. Then she waited in the darkness, hearing only the fast beat of her heart. The house seemed sound asleep.

She listened very carefully. Nothing moved or stirred.

Had Paul and Renee decided to get out with the money before the police came, she wondered. Were they already far away from the house in their car?

Johnny was lying wounded downstairs. Perhaps he was in terrible pain, lying alone and frightened.

She waited until she could wait no longer. Cautiously she moved the packing case aside. Johnny needed her. She had to go downstairs and see what she could do.

She listened again. Still no sound.

She took a deep breath and heaved the packing case completely free of the hatch. Then, still leaning against it, she waited with a fast-beating heart.

They must be away. Surely killing her wasn't so important now. Getting clear with the money before the police arrived was the most likely course of action Paul and Renee would have decided on by now.

Cautiously she knelt down beside the hatch. She hesitated

for a long moment. Then her fingers reached out to ease the hatch very slightly open so that she could peep through the crack. When it unexpectedly opened wide, her hands flew up to cover her face, to muffle a scream of anguish.

There was nothing more she could do, she was trapped, completely defenceless.

'Kirsty, it's all right. It's me. Greg.'

'Greg, oh thank God!' Her screwed up muscles relaxed. 'I thought for a dreadful moment it was Paul.'

'Don't worry. My police pals were bundling him and his partner in crime into the police car while I was looking for you.'

He shone the powerful beam of his torch from one end of the loft to the other. Its yellow beam picked out the made-up camp bed, the little table beside it, the flasks and dirty dishes, newspapers, magazines and some of Johnny's clothes.

'He was here all the time, wasn't he?'

'Greg, he came to me desperately needing help. I couldn't turn him away.'

For a brief second, Greg's big hand rested comfortingly on hers. Then he quickly disappeared back down the loft ladder.

'Come on, Kirsty,' he whispered. 'Right now, Johnny needs medical attention. There's a policeman with him and an ambulance on its way.'

Johnny was still lying on the floor where he'd fallen, with a police officer kneeling by his side trying to stem the flow of blood by pressing on his wound with a pad. Kirsty gave a sob of distress when she saw him.

'Oh Greg, shouldn't you lift him onto the settee?'

'No, darling. We mustn't move him.'

Kirsty and Greg knelt down on the other side of Johnny. Johnny opened his eyes and looked at them.

'Don't worry now.' Greg's voice was surprisingly gentle. 'Everything will be all right. The ambulance is on its way.'

Johnny managed a faint ghost of a smile.

'No, I'm already dead and it's better for everyone, including myself, if we leave it that way. Look after my Kirsty, won't you, Greg. She's always looked after me so well.'

'Of course. You know I will. But you mustn't talk like this, Johnny.'

But Johnny had turned his head towards his sister and wasn't listening to Greg any more.

'Kirsty . . .'

'Yes, dear?' She smoothed back his dark hair.

'Thanks,' he said, and his smile was loving. 'Thanks for everything.'

Then he closed his eyes.

'Oh, no, Johnny. No . . .'

The tears came all at once – pouring, streaming, tumbling down her face.

'Sh, sh, darling, please.' Greg's strong arm encircled her, held her very close. 'He wanted it this way. Look at him. See his face. He's at peace now.'

Kirsty looked at her brother. And she saw the truth of Greg's words. She nodded and tried to wipe the tears away. At least Johnny would never suffer any more.

'From now on, you've no need to worry,' Greg said. 'I'll see to everything. There will be a quiet private funeral. Your mother need never know anything about it, or any of this. Do you hear me, Kirsty? She'll be away on holiday at your Aunt Jess's cottage up north. I'll see to it. I'll arrange everything.'

# 34

Words crackled and trembled all day.

'Fire service . . .'

'There's a terrible fire . . .'

'Fire service . . .'

'The whole house is ablaze . . .'

'Fire service . . .'

'My invalid mother is trapped in her room. The door's on fire. She's screaming and I can't get in to help her.'

'Fire service . . .'

'There's flames all around us. There's me and the children here . . . Oh God . . .'

'Fire service . . .'

Greg's work helped burn away past unease, past suspicions, and now more recent, dangerous and shocking events. The suspicion that something was going on but not knowing what. The shock of finding out. The efforts to protect the Price family. Telling Simon Price what had happened. They had succeeded in hiding the bloodstains on the sitting-room carpet from Mrs Price by covering them with a rug. With Simon's help and cooperation, they had got her safely away to Simon's cheerful sister, Jess, for a holiday, where Mrs Price's attention was diverted to all the talk and preparations for the wedding, including putting the finishing touches to Kirsty's dress. She shared a bedroom with Aunt Jess and was able to stop taking the strong sedation that had previously knocked her out every night. Instead, she enjoyed chatting to Aunt Jess until they both fell asleep.

There were still the desperate attempts by everyone to hide newspapers and every form of news from Mrs Price. There was blessed relief when their efforts were successful. Indeed, the holiday was so successful and Mrs Price and Aunt Jess got on so well together that Aunt Jess decided to sell her cottage up north and move in with the Prices, to live permanently in Botanic Crescent.

'To tell the truth,' she said, 'it's been a lonely life for me, living in such an isolated spot, since I was widowed.'

All their efforts had been successful, yet Greg knew that it would take much longer for the nightmare of it all to be completely forgotten.

Sometimes Kirsty would wake up with a sudden cry of anguish and he had to hold her tightly in his arms, stroke her hair, whisper soothing words.

'It's all right. It's over. It's all over.'

But he knew how she was feeling and he was glad he had his job to blot out his nightmares.

'Fire service . . .'

'For God's sake, come quickly. There's been a terrible explosion . . .'

'Fire service . . .'

'There's flames shooting out a window of a tower block . . .'

'Fire service . . .'

'Oh my God, my children are in the bedroom. It's on fire and I can't get the door open. Oh dear Jesus, my children, my children . . .'

'Fire service . . .'

# 35

Everyone agreed that it was great that Betty and Hamish had become an item. Both of them were so happy, they could hardly take their eyes off each other. And outside of the Life class, they chatted practically non-stop. They managed to concentrate on their work inside the art class because they both knew, as they all did, that it was vitally important to have good work ready for the show in the desperate hope that they would be awarded a degree.

However, on Sundays, Betty and Hamish travelled around. They'd been to Edinburgh a couple of times already, because, as Betty said, 'There's so many fascinating things to see there and Hamish knows all the history and everything.'

'Well, not all the history and not everything,' Hamish laughed. 'But I do have an interest in Scottish history, right enough.'

Every Monday at break time, the rest of the class was regaled with their weekend adventures.

Hamish said, 'Betty's particularly interested in poets and writers. Even more so than the artists of a place. I could hardly drag her away from the Poetry Library.'

'Oh, I'm interested in the artists too. In fact, I'd love to paint some of the buildings and views I've seen in Edinburgh. It's such a beautiful city, even just to walk through and admire.'

'You wouldn't have thought it so beautiful to walk through in the early days. When it got dark, the closes would echo with the words "gardy loo" and then everybody would empty their chamber pots out of the windows.'

'Och well, I suppose most big cities would do things like that when they'd no sanitation. But I'd rather think of what I read that one citizen said of the old town, "Here I stand at what is called the Cross of Edinburgh, and can in a few minutes take fifty men of genius and learning by the hand."'

Tommy spoke up then. 'There were plenty of clever men in Glasgow. Mostly in business and trade, I suppose. Tobacco lords made Glasgow. And if you're interested in poets, Betty, you'll know what Burns said about Glasgow.'

Betty shook her head. 'No.'

'Well, there used to be a John Smith's bookshop in St Vincent Street in Burns's time, and he had some dealings with them and discovered they gave him a much better deal than the booksellers in Edinburgh. He said, "They're right decent booksellers in Glasgow, but oh they're sair birkies in Edinburgh."'

Betty laughed, and Tommy added, 'There's a plaque at the Virginia Street side of Marks & Spencer's in Argyle Street. It used to be the Black Bull Inn on that site and Robert Burns stayed there when he visited Glasgow.'

'Gosh, I must go and have a look at that.'

Sandra shook her head. 'Have you never even been around Glasgow, Betty?'

'No, just to and from the Art School. I was a prisoner in my mother's house, I realise now. That's why I'm enjoying freedom so much.' She gazed adoringly round at Hamish, oblivious to the fact that he had pimples and he was a bit overweight. 'And I'm so lucky.'

'Well, if your mother gets better,' Sandra said, 'don't you allow her to make you a prisoner again.'

'Oh, don't worry. I've learned my lesson. Nothing and no one will ever do that to me again. I'm a completely different person now.'

'Well, I think we could all agree with that. Here, look at the time! We'd better get back to work.'

They all hurried back to the art room as fast as they could. Only Tommy dragged his feet. Sandra had been quite cheered for a few minutes because Tommy had contributed to the conversation. He had got so much worse recently and hardly spoke at all, even to her.

He no longer showed any interest in painting her, and now even in the art class he just sat for most of the time staring hopelessly, miserably, at his canvas without even lifting a brush. Simon Price was away teaching a course down south, but they had heard that he was due back soon. Sandra dreaded his return, for Tommy's sake. Personally, she didn't care a button for Simon Price, or what he said. At least, she didn't care what he said to her. But oh, she wished with all her heart that she could say something or do something to stop him picking on Tommy again.

She'd spoken to Tommy about how she felt.

'I don't care what he says to me, Tommy. Why do you care what he says to you? For pity's sake, have some faith in yourself. Since that monster has been away, the other tutor hasn't criticised you or your work, has he?'

Tommy shook his head.

'Well then. It's just Simon Price's horrible nature. I've told you before. He only picks on you so much because he's a bully and you let him get away with bullying you.'

Tommy shook his head again.

'Why? Why are you letting him do this to you, Tommy? Honestly, I could shake you, anything to get you to see sense.'

'We've been over all this before, Sandra. You know perfectly well why I'm depressed. Simon Price is a brilliant artist. He knows talent when he sees it and he doesn't see any talent in my work. I respect him for being so straightforward and truthful.'

'Oh God,' Sandra groaned. 'When will you ever learn? I told you, everyone has told you, that you're a brilliant artist. You have enormous talent.'

'Simon Price knows what he's talking about.'

'And we don't? Oh, thanks very much.'

Tommy didn't say any more and, feeling depressed herself now, Sandra also fell silent. What else could she do? She had tried everything. But nothing had been any use. At least Tommy already had enough work to put into the show. Maybe once he got his degree, his self-confidence would return. She had never been a religious girl, but now she found herself praying.

'Oh God, please look after Tommy and make him see that he is a very talented artist. Please help him to get out of this terrible depression he's suffering from. I'll suffer anything for his sake. I'd rather not get my degree if it would mean he would get his and make him more confident and happy again. Please, oh please, don't let Simon Price torment him any more. Let him torment me instead and leave Tommy alone. Oh please, please, God. Help Tommy.'

# 36

'There's plenty of interesting history about Glasgow as well as Edinburgh,' Hamish told Betty.

'Glasgow used to be a wee fishing village. Although even then it had a stone cathedral. St Kentigern settled in Glasgow and called it Glas-cu. That meant the dear green place.'

'The dear green place,' Betty echoed with pleasure.

'He became Glasgow's patron saint. He was so popular that people called him Mungo. That meant dear one.'

They were walking arm in arm through Glasgow Green.

'Women used to do their washing here and dry their clothes. Can you imagine clothes flapping about in the wind all over the Green?'

'Didn't they have sinks and water in their houses?'

Hamish shrugged. 'There was a Town Council order in . . . I think it was as far back as 1623, outlawing the washing of clothes anywhere other than in private houses. But no one paid any attention. It carried on as a public washing green until 1977.' Hamish pointed ahead. 'You can still see the iron posts for ropes over there.'

Betty gazed round at him in admiration. 'I'm amazed at how much you know about history, Hamish.'

He gave a half laugh. 'Oh, I always had plenty of time to read up about it. I practically lived in libraries. The first thing I did when I found myself in a new town or wherever was to find the nearest library. It was a nice warm place to sit as well.'

He laughed again.

'By the way, the English visitors to the city all went to look at the washing being done.'

'Why on earth was that?'

'Well, the washerwomen used to stamp on the washing with their bare feet and hold up their skirts as they were doing it. That was something no one ever saw south of the border, apparently.'

Betty laughed along with him.

'So it was the bare feet and legs they came to watch.'

'Then it became the place for all sorts of games and sports. An open-air gymnasium, a golf club, a bowling green, a tennis courts, a hockey pitch, and always there was football. That's where and how Rangers Football Club started. And of course, it was like Hyde Park in London with all its preachers and politicians and all sorts of speakers bawling the odds every Saturday and Sunday.'

'It all sounds fascinating.'

'Yes, I enjoyed reading about Glasgow Green. The powers that be often tried to take it over for one commercial reason or another, but each time, the people of Glasgow fought them for the right to keep it as a public park for the use of every Glaswegian. And they always won. Now it's not only the oldest public park in Glasgow, but the oldest public park in the whole of Britain.'

'Hamish,' Betty said suddenly, 'would you like to come back home with me for tea and to meet my mother?'

'Gosh, from what you've told me about your mother, she's not going to be pleased to see me.'

'I've told her about you and said I was going to invite you. And I admit she looked furious but she always looks furiously at me now. She's obviously full to overflowing with hatred of me. She'll hate you even more. She's always loathed and detested anyone of the male sex.'

'Well, then . . .'

'Well, I'm always honest with her now. I try to be as kind as I can, but totally honest. I need to have my own life now. I think I have a right. She controlled me and made me live a lie for so long. Too long. Will you come, Hamish?'

He squeezed her arm. 'Of course I will. We'll face her together.'

'Oh, thank you, Hamish.'

They made their way then to a bus that would take them along Great Western Road to Anniesland Cross, near Betty's home. Once there, he followed her into a clean and well-maintained close, so different from his own. Betty opened the door and led Hamish along the lobby and into the sitting room. Her mother was sitting watching television. She turned a malevolent stare on them.

'Mother, this is Hamish I was telling you about.'

Hamish went over with his hand outstretched to shake the older woman's hand. He jerked quickly back when she spat at him.

Betty said, 'I told you what a nasty, horrible old woman she was but even I didn't realise she'd be that bad. I'm so sorry, Hamish.'

He shrugged and wiped the spittle off his jacket with a handkerchief.

'It's OK. Don't worry.'

'Come on through to the kitchen with me and I'll put the kettle on and make us a pot of tea.'

In the kitchen she said, 'I know you're miserable in your digs, Hamish, and I was going to suggest that you move in here but now I suppose you'll think that here would be even worse for you. But you must be disgusted by my mother's behaviour.'

'Well, yes, but I could put up with your mother, Betty, and I'd love to live with you . . .'

'Oh Hamish . . .' Betty interrupted, throwing her arms around his neck in delight.

'But wait a minute. I wouldn't move in with you unless we were married first. I had enough of the insecure kind of life my mother led. She never married, never seemed to want to settle down anywhere with anyone for any length of time. I vowed I would never be like that. I'd like a happy, settled life with a wife and family. And I'd make sure my family had a secure and loving home life. That's always been my dream.'

Betty's face glowed with happiness.

'Was that a proposal, Hamish?'

He grinned. 'I suppose it was.'

'Well, the answer's yes.'

'But we'd have to get our degrees first and decent jobs so that we'd manage OK financially.'

'Yes, of course. I thought of teaching. I mean, it's pretty precarious to try to live on any paintings I'd be able to sell at first. Teaching would give the security of a regular wage while I try to get established as an artist. What were you thinking?'

'Much the same.'

'Is that what we'll do then?'

'OK. I guess that's it settled. All being well with our degrees, we should have no problem getting into teacher training and now that they guarantee you a job for your probation year, that would make a good start.'

It wasn't until much later, after Hamish had gone back to his digs, that Betty realised that it wouldn't be fair to subject him to full-time ghastly treatment by her mother. Their marriage wouldn't stand a chance with the constant barrage of hatred and every kind of abuse her mother would hurl at them.

In the end, Betty decided that the best thing for all

concerned was to get her mother into a good care home or nursing home where she'd have proper health care and supervision. She could apply to a private place because her mother had been left plenty of money by Betty's father. And once her mother was in care, the NHS would, Betty believed, take on the burden of payment when her mother's money ran out.

Betty contacted her local doctor, social services and even the Citizens' Advice, and was promised help and someone to come out and assess the extent of the problem. She was told, however, that there should be no problem in getting a placement if things were as bad as she claimed with her mother's infirmity and mental health problems.

'I'll come and visit you, Mother,' she assured her.

An appointment was made for a carer and social worker to visit, with a view to a possible placement in a care home in Summerston, which was not too far away, and Betty had had good reports of its reputation.

She couldn't help it – the thought of having the house free of her mother's hatred was incredible. It was so wonderful, she did a wild dance around each room. She told Hamish but he stuck to his determination not to move in with her until after they were both awarded their degrees.

She prayed that they would succeed in getting their degrees. Soon they would know. Oh, life could not be so cruel as to make her fail. Not now. They had both worked so hard. She just knew everything was going to be all right. Oh, how happy she was! She was dancing in her mind:

Every step I take this morning
lands on a cushion of air.
All we did last night was kiss
and today you flavour everything
my mind touches.

Your voice sounds in the rumble
of a passing car. The valerian blue
of your eyes swims on top of a puddle,
promising birds safety
and a place to bathe.

A boy with short, brown hair
gelled to spikes, holds his mother's hand
while crossing the road. I see you
in the way his eyes tug at her,
checking she is still there.
He gives a little kick with each step
as if the promise of a future
nips at his heels.

An old man at the bus stop, round
like Santa. You in fifty years. Cheeks
bunched in a grin, wearing an apple blush
like you last night when you brushed
my right breast with your arm.

Caught myself smiling at him,
wanting to know
how we carry the years,
yet don't want to spoil the dance
of every blood cell
through the chambers of my heart,
like millions of tiny breeze-blown flowers.

# 37

He was back. Sandra could see Tommy visibly shrink even before Simon Price said a word to him. It was not only painful to look at Tommy's hopelessness and depression; she was suffering the pain of it as well. She couldn't bear to see Tommy like this. She hated Simon Price for ruining both their lives. They had once been carefree and happy together. So full of plans for the future. Tommy was a sensitive and brilliantly talented young man with everything to live for, to hope for. It was wicked that he had been reduced to this. The course was nearing its end. All of their work, including Tommy's, was ready for the show. They were all on tenterhooks about whether or not they would get their degree. Tommy had lost every vestige of hope that he would get his.

Then Simon Price said he hadn't a chance in hell.

'You?' he sneered. 'No way!'

Just after he'd said that, Price was giving them a last lecture about Charles Rennie Mackintosh and leading them around the building, explaining Mackintosh's thinking and intentions behind the architecture of the place.

'He purposefully made some areas dark to make a contrast with the lighter areas. Like this dark part which leads on to the light area of the "hen run" and makes that light all the more startling. If we . . .'

Just then, Tommy unexpectedly raced over to a metal ladder, clambered up it and pushed at the hatch above.

'What the hell?'

Before Sandra could even think what was happening, Simon Price had raced after him. In what seemed a matter of seconds, Tommy had pulled himself through the hatch and out onto the roof. The wind whipped at his T-shirt, moulding it to his slender body. He staggered at first, leaning into the wind to catch his balance. Beyond and below, the rooftops of Glasgow spread out like a patchwork blanket as far as the horizon, and a shiny sliver of the Clyde sparkled at the edge of his vision, the only sounds the rushing of the wind and the slight, far-away hum of the traffic on Sauchiehall Street below.

He turned precariously round, his arms spread wide for balance, and called back down through the open hatch, 'I'm sorry, Sandra. I'm no use. I can't stand it. I can't go on, I just can't any more. I'm going to jump. I can't take any more of Price's torture.'

'Calm down, Pratt. Tommy, I'm sorry,' Price called. Visions of tomorrow's papers flashed through his mind, with no doubts about who would play the villain of the piece.

'You're a brilliant artist,' Price called up through the hatch. Price slowly levered himself up, head and shoulders through the hatch, his hands gripping the lead guttering firmly.

'Come on, Tommy. You're over-reacting. Yes, I've been hard on you, maybe too hard. OK, I can be a bastard but I've only been trying to toughen you up. I've had rejections and been told I was no use in my day. So have all artists. Have you never heard what Van Gogh suffered? You need to be bloody tough to survive. I had to toughen you up. You're such a brilliant artist, you have to survive for everyone else's sake. And of course you've got your degree, the same as everybody else. You've got your degree, the same as your classmates. Do you hear me?'

Slowly, gently, his voice calming as if talking to a frightened animal, he stretched out his hand.

'Please, Tommy, give me your hand and we can both come down out of here.'

There was a moment's agonising hesitation before Tommy did as he was told. Price grabbed his hand and pulled him over and down the hatch. At the foot of the stairs, he said, 'My God, don't you ever do anything like that to me again.' Then to Sandra, 'Take him home. Wrap him up and give him some hot, sweet tea. He should be OK. But just keep an eye on him and make sure you're both here early tomorrow.'

The shock of what had happened and, worse, what could have happened, robbed Sandra of her voice. Obediently, she led a grey-faced Tommy away.

'I told you,' she said eventually. 'How many times have I told you . . .'

'I know, Sandra. I've been a fool. I'm so sorry. But I thought, you see, that you were just praising me because you love me. Like I love you. And he is so talented and I just thought he must be the one I should believe as far as my art is concerned.'

'No, it's that bastard Price who's been the fool. It's not surprising you got so depressed, when he kept rubbishing you and your work. It was really wicked of him.'

'At least his intentions were good. He believed he was doing the right thing for me.'

'Bollocks! He's just a wicked bully. You let him off with it and so he went to town on you. I'm telling you, he enjoyed bullying you, that was all.'

Tommy drew Sandra into his arms.

'I appreciate your faith in me. It's really wonderful how you've always believed in me and stuck by me, Sandra. I don't deserve you.'

'There you go, knocking yourself again. I could scream at you, Tommy. Have confidence in yourself. You must from now on. Just keep thinking to yourself, "I'm a brilliant artist and I'm going to be famous, not only here, but all over the world." Make a mantra of it. Keep on saying it over and over until you've convinced yourself deep down.'

Tommy couldn't help laughing.

'You and your wild imagination.'

'Tommy!' Sandra warned.

'OK, OK. I'm a brilliant artist and I'm going to be famous, not only here, but all over the world. I'm a brilliant artist and I'm going to be famous, not only here, but all over the world.'

'That's better.'

He kissed her gently at first, then with growing passion. Later in bed, they spoke of the degrees the next day. That was the Thursday when all the officials at the Art School would be there. Then the Friday was the show, when family and friends could come and everyone would party until midnight.

They were both so excited now at the mere idea of it all, they couldn't sleep for what seemed an age. Eventually, happily exhausted, sleep overcame them.

The street was closed, from under the library all the way past the Newbery Tower and the Mackintosh building, to allow for the celebrations.

There was a small stage set up and a local indie band was blasting out music, the raucous guitar riffs bouncing off the stately walls of the Mackintosh façade. A group of students bounced around in a heaving mass in front of the band. One of the girls had jumped from the stage and was crowd-surfing, held aloft on a raft of hands. Others filled the streets in small groups, singing, dancing and generally letting their hair down. Drink flowed freely and there was a pungent sweet aroma wafting on the breeze as some of the students lit up, with little regard to where they were.

Sandra flung her hands up high, her red hair a vivid curtain swinging about over her cavorting body.

Tommy was laughing uproariously and stumbling about, trying to keep up with Sandra.

Hamish kept swinging a joyous Betty off her feet, round and round and round, making her skirts fly up and reveal glimpses of her thong.

Kirsty and Greg had been invited and were joining in with as much wild abandon as everyone else.

Kirsty believed, as they all did, that this day was the beginning of freedom and a new, wonderful and fulfilling life.

'Yeehah!' somebody yelled and the sound echoed in everyone's heart.